FREEZING DOWN

FREEZING
DOWN

Anders Bodelsen

Translated from the Danish by Joan Tate

HARPER & ROW, PUBLISHERS

New York, Evanston, San Francisco, London

1817

This work was originally published in Denmark under the title *Frysepunktet.*

FREEZING DOWN

1973

I

The telephone stands on the windowsill. Without waking up, Bruno has taken the five cold strides across the floor and is standing with the receiver in his hand. As he waits for the voice that is to tell him that he has ordered an alarm call and the time is eight o'clock, he looks at the ice crystals behind the curtain, which he has drawn aside without thinking. He wants to look at the thermometer outside the window, but he cannot because of the ice crystals. Still only half awake, he remembers how as a child he had put a coin on the radiator and then pressed it against the ice crystals to give himself a little hole he could peep through, out into a dark winter's morning like this.

There are no coins on the windowsill. Bruno leans forward and breathes on the ice crystals. After a while, he has made a dark patch in the white pattern, an opening. And another memory flits past: he is skating, alone, carelessly, on a lake at dusk. He passes quite close to a hole in the ice, stops, wants to turn back, can no longer in the half light discern where the ice will bear him and where it will not. Skates on a bit, shouts, hoping for an answer, but he is alone on the lake and it has grown dark much earlier than he had expected, and suddenly he realizes that he has been skating on very thin ice all the time and even if he skates back exactly the same way he came, if he can find it, it is not certain that the ice will bear him again.

"45 65 06 18 13?"

"Yes."

"This is your alarm call. It is eight o'clock."

"Thank you."

"Good morning."

"Good morning."

As he was shaving, Bruno cut himself. The blade struck an irregularity on his neck, and blood flowed out through the foaming suds, slowly making an almost complete garland around his neck before he washed the foam away and stanched the wound with stinging shaving lotion. At the same time, he was listening to his record of *Famous Mad Scenes.* When he had finished dressing, he went over to the window again. The little opening he had made in the ice crystals had not closed up. He enlarged it with his warm forefinger, until he could read the thermometer. It was twelve degrees above zero. Then he pushed the balcony door open, went out and stood by the railing, feeling the wind bite into his newly shaved and lotioned chin. The dark of the night was just being relieved by gray dawn. He looked down over the city and then at the other buildings on a level with his own. There were no lights in the tallest ones, for they had not yet been completed. He looked at the remaining cupolas and spires of what had once been the city's famous skyline, but that all would soon be hidden behind taller buildings. From his apartment he could see over almost the whole of the city, while

4

those on the other side of the building looked out over the harbor and the sea. The sound of a siren made Bruno look down toward the fire house at the bottom of his building. A single fire engine pulled out into the street and disappeared from sight, but he was able to hear the direction it took, toward the city center. Then *Famous Mad Scenes* came to an end and he realized that he must hurry.

He was thirty-two and walked to work to keep his weight down. His office was in another tall building, not quite as tall as the one he lived in, but nevertheless taller than most of the buildings in the city center. Bruno's office was on the ninth floor. FICTION EDITOR, it said on his door. First he used the telephone to order coffee and sweetening tablets. Then he began to call his authors.

"I've a brand-new idea for you today," he said into the mouthpiece. "Listen. A man is found murdered on a beach. We're in some holiday paradise, a little island in the Pacific, or what have you. In his hands he is clasping a newspaper from back home, and we soon find out that it's yesterday's paper and it has been flown out to the island that same day. The point is that the murderer has read the paper at home and has hurried off to the island because there was something in the paper that he could not allow his victim to read. Which, in other words, considering what the murdered man knew beforehand, would have become damning evidence. What do you think of that?"

Bruno was not the only fiction editor on this weekly magazine, but he was the man with the most ideas. Crime was his specialty, but no one had told him that he had to limit himself to his specialty. He made another phone call.

"Listen to this. A man makes his living by selling cars. Every evening he makes sure that it is he who puts the lights out and locks up. Then he drives the most expensive car in the place up along the coast and spends all his money at the most expensive hotels, where he makes out he is all kinds of exciting people. Combined perhaps with the idea of a wig which changes a bald man so that he is unrecognizable, psychologically too. Try and see if those two ideas don't fertilize each other. I think they will. Perhaps something about him beginning to win at roulette too. Or is that too much of a good thing?"

A number of Bruno's authors were quite dependent on him. Either they no longer had any ideas themselves, or else they combined the ideas they had in the wrong way. Bruno knew what each author was capable of, and quite often he took ideas from one and passed them on to another, or simply got them to exchange ideas.

"I've a new twist to that idea we talked about the other day—the man who commits a murder and then flees the country, but who is so homesick that he defies good sense and goes back to his native country and his friends in disguise. *What* disguise? you asked me then. Hold on a moment—why not as a woman? Why not a spot of humor? I think you in particular have the necessary tact, or whatever you like to call it, to use that idea without it becoming distasteful. What do you think?"

After an hour's brainstorming on the telephone, Bruno paused awhile before getting on with his routine work of correcting manuscripts. He was capable of seeing his prolificity in a humorous light. It was somewhat unnatural to have so many ideas and then only distribute them among others. Sometimes, when Bruno waxed especially enthusiastic about one of his ideas, an author might ask him why he didn't try to use it himself. Bruno had promised himself that he would do so one day; one day when he had an idea that was wholly original. He had no illusions about most of his ideas; they

6

could be used, but they were in no way remarkable. Anyway, the work was more important than the idea itself. Good stories could be written around mediocre ideas and a good idea could be ruined by a bad author. For one reason or another, Bruno's best ideas often ended as stories that were so poor that they were hardly publishable. Someday he wished to find out for himself whether his best ideas were not better than what materialized when his authors made use of them.

An illustrator had made the girl in a kidnapping story black-haired instead of blond, and Bruno had to go through the whole story to make sure that the girl was black-haired in the text. He could have phoned the illustrator and got him to correct the drawings, but it was easier to change the text. The girl was so black-haired that Bruno decided to give her a Jewish name—Rachel—a beautiful name that he could not remember using before. He was aware of the slight absurdity of his work, as he looked up all the places where her name and hair color were mentioned and then altered them. But after the hectic early-morning distribution of new ideas among his authors, it was quite soothing to do such painstakingly routine work.

After lunch in the canteen at the top of the building, Bruno spent an hour writing résumés, headings and captions for illustrations. Then he dictated letters, following up the morning's telephone calls and reiterating his ideas. At three o'clock he went to a meeting, at which he revealed his plans for the summer's crime stories, gave an account of the short story situation and entered into a discussion of principles regarding the permissible degree of erotic frankness in love stories. Bruno was in favor of greater frankness, not only because he felt forced to follow current trends, but also because this was his personal conviction. Bruno had been appointed because a new manager had been in favor of quality. At the moment, the magazine's circulation was going up, despite competition from the other mass media. Bruno listened to himself as he spoke. The day had started in a slightly unusual way, with two exceptional and clear memories from his childhood occurring, as he had stood there on the cold floor by the telephone. He heard how convincingly he was making his opinions felt; at the same time it struck him that some of what he had remembered by the telephone might be usable, might be turned into literary ideas.

That evening he went to dinner at the home of one of his authors. Bruno embraced the author's wife, kissed her on both cheeks and handed her the twelve yellow roses he had bought on his way home from work. Before dinner they had a cocktail, which almost swept him off his feet. The company was small, and Bruno looked around to see which single lady had been invited for him. At the table he had a woman psychiatrist on his left, but she was married; on his right was a shy dark girl, whose first name he had caught and taken the trouble to remember as he had been introduced: Jenny. He knew the psychiatrist and was slightly afraid of her. He felt that she was putting something more into his words, when he talked about his work and his ideas, than he did himself. She made him feel that he was a case; that it was not his work and ideas which really interested her, but the motives which drove him to tell her about them. He turned to his other table companion, but she was taciturn. He had not wanted to start asking her about her occupation, but when other leads had come to nothing, that is where he ended; she was a ballet dancer, she told him.

Bruno talked shop across the table with his host. They discussed the increasing need for good stories and Bruno said that in the society of the future, and to some extent even now, anyone who could tell a good story fell into the top income bracket. The ability was rare and there was nothing unreasonable about its being well paid. Bruno felt himself being watched penetratingly by the woman psychiatrist as he presented his theories and finally began to offer several ideas across the table; the ballet dancer ate her dessert in silence.

After dinner, Bruno found himself sitting in another group. Across the room he caught a glimpse of the dancer, who was making herself useful by keeping the fire going. At half past eleven, he decided to leave. He had a feeling he had neglected the girl he had been invited to escort. He went across to her by the fire and asked if he could give her a lift home. She looked up at him and said, yes, please, if it was not too far out of his way. The author's wife embraced Bruno again and once again thanked him for the yellow roses. She looked happy and Bruno was satisfied that he had finally pulled himself together sufficiently to do something for the lady for whom he had been invited.

It was freezing outside and he had to heat the car key with his lighter before he could get it into the lock. The girl lived halfway out in a suburb and it was far out of his way, though Bruno assured her that it was not. He again asked her about her work and she spoke briefly about the difficulty of making one's name in ballet. Bruno had the impression that the girl danced nearly all day, overworking herself, and that she was perhaps on the verge of a slight depression because she was not getting anywhere in her career. She had no sense of humor whatsoever and it struck him as an attractive characteristic. She was sitting up straight, looking somewhat dejected in her thin black coat. Her hair was jet black, like the girl's in the illustration—Rachel, as Bruno had christened her after her new hair. She smelled pleasant, though not of scent, but rather of soap. She was thin and pretty in a melancholy way. Their conversation came to a halt as they approached her building. She

9

rented a room in an apartment that had become too large for an elderly couple.

Bruno felt that the girl would have liked company and would have invited him up for a drink if he had asked, but he did not ask. He said good night to her, remaining seated at the wheel while she stood outside the car. He waved as she turned into the doorway, and then started up the car. There remained a slight fragrance of her soap. On his way home, he remembered a couple of lines from an old song: "You were made to go out and get her." Or was it "meant to"? Alone in the car, he hummed the tune.

At home, the record of *Famous Mad Scenes* was still on the turntable. He switched it on and then off again. Undressing, he went on humming the old tune. He stopped again by the window and breathed on the ice crystals until there was an opening and he could look at his thermometer. The girl's second name was Holländer. Jenny Holländer. He might well have gone up with her, and perhaps ought to have done so. Holländer. Could he phone her now and ask if he might come over? He found her name in the directory. He lifted the receiver and then replaced it. He could, but he did not. Through the hole he saw that it was nine degrees above zero.

Humming, he went and looked in his bathroom mirror. "You were meant to," he sang, "go out and get her." He examined his neck where he had cut himself that morning and his finger stopped at the obstacle that the razor blade had met. With three fingers, he encircled it; a small hard ball under the skin. He remembered it being there a few days earlier, when he had been standing in front of the mirror as now, but in the meantime it had grown in size and become harder.

Bruno ran the tips of his fingers over the irregularity. He was frowning and had stopped humming.

2

Dr. Josef Ackermann felt Bruno's neck with a pair of cold fingers. The doctor had scarlet patches on his cheeks and large dark eyes. He appeared young, and was probably not much older than Bruno himself. Bruno wondered whether it would not be difficult to put trust in a man so close to himself in age.

"Yes," said Dr. Ackermann. "It seems to be some irregularities."

Bruno wondered about the plural form.

"There's another one coming. You know, I don't think it's anything to worry about too much. But I'd very much like to take a closer look at it."

Taking his hands away from Bruno's neck, he had gone back to his desk and sat down, beginning to interlock his fingers.

"I'd like to go over you from A to Z, and that can be done as an outpatient, but really it's much easier for everyone if you'd come in for a few days."

"So it's not out of the question that it's something . . . malignant," said Bruno, though he could see how unnecessary the question was.

"Not entirely. I'd very much like to have you in soon."

"Soon?"

"This afternoon."

Bruno had considered the possibility of going into a hospital, but he had not imagined that it would happen so quickly, or that a doctor would consider haste so imperative.

"I have a bed for you—I imagine you'd prefer a private room? You can have a phone put in, and there would be no objection to your bringing some of your work with you."

Now that the preliminary examination was over, the doctor appeared older and more self-confident. As Bruno rose, he felt the blood rushing from his head. He clutched at the edge of Dr. Ackermann's desk and heard the doctor ask, in a voice that seemed to reach him through several rooms and doors:

"Are you all right?"

It helped to lean against something. The doctor went away and returned with a small jar of pills and a glass of water. He made Bruno swallow two yellow pills.

"Those should calm you down a little. If I were you, I wouldn't be too scared. You've done the right thing. Most people wait a longer time before going to a doctor. The likelihood is that it's not serious, and *if* it is, you've come sufficiently early that we have a good chance of clearing it up. Did you drive here?"

"Yes."

"If I were you, I'd take a taxi now. You're not quite yourself."

Following the doctor's advice, Bruno walked past his car, leaving it parked there. The hospital consisted of a new high building, which was so long that it resembled a ship, and a number of small pavilions, which the new building should

12

really have replaced, but which were still in use. The consultation had taken place on one of the new building's lower floors. The frosty air made Bruno's eyes water. When he had walked for a few minutes, he noticed that the two yellow pills were having an effect. He slowed down and thought he noticed his heart slowing down also. The sense that something inside him kept on falling vanished. He had taken the most important and most difficult step; he had been to the doctor and in that way shed the responsibility. Now he had earned the luxury of getting through the rest of the day with the help of heated taxis.

The sun was shining and it was a beautiful frosty day. He took a taxi to the office, hunching up a little on the seat as a sick man may allow himself to do, but all the same now and again looking out at the sunlit city through the window, wiping it clean with his gloved hand.

At the office, he collected five manuscripts of stories he had postponed reading and yet another that had come in the morning mail. Before he could leave, there was a telephone call for him, an author with no ideas. Bruno hesitated at first, because he realized that he was affected by the yellow pills, but then he began to speak.

"It's an old chestnut, but perhaps it just about merits a new round. The ballet dancer who finds it hard to make her name. Is obliged to sleep with her ballet master to get a role. Try modernizing it. She *does* it. In the old days, she didn't. She goes to bed with him and later becomes terribly depressed. Read up about depressions, purely psychological. It's not an idea, I know. But it's perhaps what I usually call an idea for an idea."

The author did not think much of his idea or the idea for an idea, so Bruno suggested that he write about a man who becomes addicted to automobile-racing and how his wife wins

13

him back by beating him in cross-country rallies. Then Bruno left, manuscripts under each arm and the rest of his routine work distributed among the other fiction editors. He took another taxi to his apartment.

The yellow pills were still working. From his window, the city was more beautiful than he remembered ever seeing it. The sunlight was pouring into his room and it fell on his shelves of books and records, and on *Famous Mad Scenes*, still on the phonograph. The last time he had played it, things had been ordinary and he had been healthy. He did not put on any music, but made himself a cup of tea as he packed his suitcase. Then he became aware that the effect of the yellow pills was wearing off. The sun had gone around the corner and was now flooding the doors of the cupboards that divided the kitchen area from the rest of the room, and then it had gone altogether and the room suddenly seemed strangely menacing. He realized that there was not a single person whom he wished to tell about his disease, if it was a disease. No colleague at work, none of the girls he knew. Not the layout girl he had occasionally brought back home; not any of his authors or authoresses. He was alone with his knowledge—he and Dr. Ackermann. He took two yellow pills with the last of the cold tea, rinsed out the cup and left.

In the lobby, where he arranged for his mail to be forwarded as he waited for his third taxi of the day, he noticed again that he was able to relax. Once more, he had the feeling that he had shed all responsibility.

He got the taxi to drive a long route through the city. The sun was low, the city full of busy people, a story in every one of them, a story that could be told and used. It was a feeling he had often had ten or fifteen years ago; reality is full of stories and all one need do is to gather them up. His authors made a mess of the stories he presented to them, in some way

14

or another always draining them of the life, the reality they ought to have contained. Bruno should have written the best stories himself. He ought to have taken himself more seriously.

The light of the setting sun fell on him through the front window and the glass partition between himself and the driver. Bruno lifted his hands into the cold sunlight for a moment. There are no new stories, he thought, but at this particular moment he felt a desire to write one of the old ones himself. A man has reason to believe that he is going to die. The world changes and improves while he awaits his doom. Traditionally, in these stories, the doctor has muddled the X-ray plates and in the last chapter the man returns to life, his senses all alert. The reader doesn't think of asking what happened to the man with the *other* X-ray plates, the one who thought he was going to live. Could one write a double story about them both? Or just about the other one?

The taxi drove into the hospital grounds as dusk fell. Bruno was given a room in one of the old pavilions, with a view of the new building. The bed smelled fresh and pleasant; he got up for the evening meal, and then went back to bed, where he lay reading a story about a woman minister in a difficult rural parish. After one or two pages, he knew he would reject the manuscript, but he read on; it was so bad it fascinated him.

An assistant doctor wrote down his particulars and Bruno's quite normal pulse and temperature were taken. It was nine o'clock and he read for another hour. The pills had made him sleepy, but he felt he could not allow himself to put the light out before ten o'clock.

Just before he fell asleep, two clear thoughts came to the surface: they had brought him in in great haste; he had no one in the world in whom he would like to confide. Why not? Twice in the last forty-eight hours he had almost admitted that his work was absurd. Was his whole life also absurd, and was it only four yellow pills that had prevented him from seeing this during the course of the day?

A cart on which something was rattling was being pushed along the corridor. A bell rang in the distance, and water or steam hissed in a pipe up under the ceiling. Bruno closed his eyes and drove in a taxi through long streets in the frosty light.

3

The next day began with blood tests and no breakfast. Bruno had been told that he must not drink so much as a glass of water after midnight. A woman in a white coat came and drew some blood from his earlobes—a small amount—and then enough to fill several test tubes from a vein in his arm. After this bloodletting, Bruno felt faint and thirsty. He had hoped for an encouraging glimpse of Dr. Ackermann, but he had been left alone with a morning paper, which he forced himself to read.

At nine o'clock they gave him an injection, and at half past nine he was, just like a real patient, pushed along long cold corridors to an operating room. The injection made him feel distant and caused him to study the ceilings hovering by with rather more interest than the back of the porter's neck.

In the operating room, or the anteroom to it, he received, as he had hoped, a prick in his arm. Just before he lost consciousness, he caught a glimpse of Dr. Ackermann with his red cheeks and lively young eyes—Dr. Ackermann was just putting on a pixie cap of the same blue color as his gown.

Someone was patting his cheeks and he was half awake. Again he studied the ceilings in the cold passages, and then he was alone in his room with his newspaper, two biscuits and an invalid cup of fruit juice and water. It was snowing on the other side of the window, and behind the snow rose the shiplike building, its lights on in the middle of the day—it was a quarter to twelve. A piece of tape, nothing more, had been put on his neck. His loins hurt slightly and his fingers found their way to yet another piece of tape, just below his chest.

Next time he woke up, it had stopped snowing and someone had exchanged the juice for a cup of tea, already grown cold and bitter. He sat up in bed.

The injection's effect had worn off and he discovered that his hands were trembling violently. When he voluntarily shook his right hand, it went on trembling of its own accord. He had to grasp it with his left hand to stop them both from shaking.

At half past one, he felt fully conscious. Dr. Ackermann appeared, glanced at his normal pulse and temperature, and encouragingly pressed his ankle through the bedcover. Bruno was given permission to get up and sit in the chair by the window. There were a hundred things he wished to ask about, but he knew it was too soon and did not ask about anything.

At half past two, an assistant doctor gave Bruno permission to go out for an afternoon walk. He had finished the story about the woman minister and had begun another, a more exciting one, but just as unusable. An author tells a colleague about a brilliant idea he has had for a crime story. Author Two murders Author One and becomes rich and famous from the idea. Then Author One's lady friend appears. Author One, it seems, had written his version of the story and given her the manuscript before he died. Blackmail, a back-to-front love

18

story between the girl and Author Two, masses of material, but the story had two weaknesses: it did not tell you the brilliant idea; and people would not, Bruno was quite certain, stand any more stories about authors and novels. Although Bruno once more felt entertained, he put the manuscript to one side and looked at his hands, which had begun to tremble again as soon as he thought about them. Then he went out into the passage to tell the nurse that he was going out for his afternoon walk.

The people he met in the hospital grounds were wearing black hospital robes or were hurrying away in thin coveralls. Bruno found a side gate and walked briskly on. He thrust his hands into his pockets, where they no longer trembled, as long as he clenched them hard enough. At first he gave no thought to the direction in which he was going, then he saw that he was heading for the district where a day and a half ago he had dropped off his quiet table companion, the ballet dancer. Why? Because the ballet idea was a good one and demanded a little more research? Perhaps. There was no harm in keeping oneself occupied while one awaited one's sentence.

He came to her street—a long dark street with too narrow a space between the two rows of facades, a street where the snow was already dirty—and he hurried down it. Could he look her up and tell her that he wanted to use her life as material for a magazine story? He could hardly do that, and it struck him that the injection he had had that morning must still be having an effect.

The point was, he thought, that there was no one in the whole world whom he had a desire to see now. He ran into someone on the pavement and was frightened. The street and the pedestrians, the parked cars, the traffic and the low cloud ceiling, full of more snow to come, seemed menacing to him. A shop at basement level attracted his attention, its window full of dummy boxes of chocolates and packets of cigars, the posters for newspapers and magazines frightening him with their dreariness. Suddenly he was not sure that he could get through another minute without speaking to someone. Then he was standing outside her building and he went upstairs without thinking about how he was going to start a conversation if she was at home.

She was not. It was an elderly lady who opened the door, undoing the safety chain after looking at him, and telling him that Miss Holländer usually came home from her practice just after four. It was a quarter to, so he went down to the street again.

It was no longer any use clenching his fists in his pockets. In the basement shop he bought a light ale, then opened it with his pocketknife in a doorway and drank it. His hands stopped trembling so fiercely. When he went out onto the street again, dusk had fallen. He walked up and down the sidewalk near her building for half an hour. He contemplated taking a taxi to get back to the hospital as quickly as possible, then realized that he had not enough money on him for the fare. Could he drive right in and get a nurse to pay for it? As he was considering this, he caught sight of Jenny Holländer walking along the pavement toward him.

She smiled when she saw him; he could not remember seeing her smile before.

"Are you looking for me?"

"Yes, I am, as a matter of fact. What about a cup of tea?" He felt no sense of pushing himself in.

"You found her?" said the landlady, when Jenny had let them into the building. Then there was a surprise. From the dark hall, smelling of cabbage and stale tobacco smoke, a spiral staircase ran up one floor, to an attic room that got its light from two large skylights. It seemed lighter than outside.

It was roomy and there was furniture along only one of the walls—a sofa, a small dressing table, a tape recorder, shelves for records and ballet books. The opposite wall was covered with a long full-length mirror. On the third wall, where the light from the two attic windows gathered as in a prism, there was a rail. The fourth wall was decorated with a number of huge photographic enlargements. Bruno looked at them and saw that the pictures were of Jenny, two of them in rehearsal costume and the third in classical ballet costume.

"Yes, that's me," said Jenny, smiling.

"What are you dancing? In that one in the costume?"

"*Coppelia.* I've studied the part and I'm a kind of understudy, at the moment, if the person who's got it should happen to be ill or anything like that. Unfortunately, she's as strong as a horse. Do you know *Coppelia?*"

"I've seen it. Is it your favorite role?"

"One of them. It's exciting to dance like a mechanical doll. To be *on the point* of coming alive all the time. Did you want a cup of tea?"

There was something about the room's overilluminated narcissism that Bruno found hard to connect with this thin, solemn girl. Nothing in the room gave the impression that she would be interested in anything but dancing, and, in the final analysis, herself, her body.

"Yes, please," said Bruno.

Jenny put the water on a hot plate over by the tape recorder. She laid the little Formica-covered table in front of the sofa with tea things and candles. They waited for the water to boil and sat down.

"How nice that you were passing. Tell me what you want. Not that you *have* to want anything."

She had said the word "nice," it occurred to Bruno, very conventionally, as if she did not connect the concept of niceness and comfort with anything that might belong in this bare room, where everything was arranged to give floor space. But she had also said it in a very friendly way. The water boiled, and she turned her back on him for a moment.

"Promise me you won't be offended," he began.

She promised him, glancing over her shoulder. The tea was to draw for five minutes and she carefully set a small alarm clock and came back to him on the sofa.

"You see, I work for a weekly magazine," he began.

She nodded seriously. Then he told her of his idea for a story about a ballet dancer. Just as he had finished explaining, the alarm clock rang and she went to get the tea. He could not make out if she was disappointed or offended because he simply wanted to pump her for material. But when she came back and poured out the tea, she looked happy, and over the tea she began to tell him freely about her life, or rather her work, with a fervor that reassured him. He had been neither obtrusive nor tactless. She was pleased to tell him about her troubles. He had no need to give her cues.

He realized that he had not explained to her that he did not write himself, that he just had ideas and gave them to other people. He managed to insert it into her stream of words, but the distinction did not seem to interest her—the distinction between having ideas and using them. Just as he had thought, her greatest difficulty was that she never got any roles, never had the remotest chance of showing what she could do, if she did not feel inclined to sleep with this person or that. Not being born and bred in the city was also a disadvantage. He guessed that her crushing solemnity was a third handicap; he could only imagine her dancing a very severe part.

As they sat there they could observe themselves in the mirror above. He saw in the mirror when she raised her teacup, forgetting to drink the tea in her eagerness to talk. She put the teacup down without having drunk any. He saw himself looking toward the mirror, saw her, in the mirror, observe this. He turned toward her quickly and said, "Yes?" because for the first time she was about to stop.

The dusk that had fallen over the narrow street had now also reached this high attic room, the two candles and their illuminated faces and their two white teacups gradually becoming the only things he could see in the mirror when he glanced in that direction again. Her story was long and banal. There was nothing in it that he could not have guessed or written better himself. Gradually she spoke more and more slowly, repeating some of what she had already told him and finally pulling herself up short.

"Are *you* unhappy about something?" she asked.

He shook his head and tried to smile. "Why do you think that?"

"You suddenly looked so sad. Perhaps that's because I'm sitting here telling you sad things. What have you done to your neck?"

"Cut myself shaving. You're not offended at my coming here and pumping you for material in this way?"

"Of course not. It's nice to be able to talk about one's work."

She glanced at his hands; he had been sitting kneading them together for some time.

"Tell me," he said, "have you anything outside your work?"

"Outside it?"

"Besides ballet, art?"

"Have *you*?" she asked.

He nodded. "But there's a difference. You can't really live *for* my work. Yours . . ."

". . . you can only just live off it. If you don't live for it, you're lost."

She chose her words with care. She said "lost" as if it really

23

meant that the foundations slid away from under everything that needed foundations. Bruno had never met a person who spoke with such seriousness; her solemnity both scared and attracted him, and he thought, as he had thought two evenings earlier when he had driven her home in his car, that she was on the edge of a depression. She was hanging on by a thin thread. And at the same time he thought, or it struck him: foundation . . . thread . . . Watch—as he said to his authors —watch that you don't mix your metaphors too much.

"You live *for* your art?"

"You make it sound so serious."

"And isn't it?"

"Yes," she said, lowering her eyes.

It occurred to him that their conversation had taken a melodramatic turn—melodramatic, or simplified, or sentimental enough to make him wish to remove it from a story. That kind should be *shown;* dialogue is an emergency solution, he would have said to one of his authors. People who talk never talk about anything important. One uses dialogue to show that people beat about the bush. Hand it over in print to the reader to find out *what* bush it is they are beating about. The reader loves to be given small, simple tasks.

The thought silenced him: was his theory wrong? Jenny poured out more tea and switched on the tape recorder. *Coppelia,* one of the very few ballets of which Bruno knew the music.

"You *are* unhappy about something," repeated Jenny stubbornly. She was standing in the middle of the empty floor in a pretty posture and Bruno imagined that she suddenly wanted to do a couple of dance steps, destroying his picture of her. But she came back to the sofa with quite ordinary steps.

"Fortunately, I may dance here," she said, "but not everyone is so lucky with their rooms. You must put that in too.

The little gray dancing mouse has permission to listen to the music in her solitary den, but dance to it she may not."

He smiled. "Gray dancing mouse. You underrate the weekly press. And also you underrate yourself."

"I shall have to read some weekly magazines. Promise me you'll send me a copy when *my* story comes out?"

He could not think how he was going to leave, so he stayed until half past five. Then he got up very abruptly, looked at his watch, his actions in the wrong order, and said that someone was waiting for him.

"Your authors?"

"One of them. I have many."

She went out with him. In the entrance he embraced her quickly and kissed her on both cheeks. She was small, cool, firm and muscular to hold, and he had a feeling that he would be able to dance ballet with her, that she would be able to steer him and send him away from her in the most impressive leaps. She smelled of soap again and this time perhaps slightly, in a pleasant and personal way, of sweat.

"Come again if you've forgotten anything," she said, after recovering from his surprising embrace.

Down on the street, he was allowed into a florist's that was really closed. He couldn't think of anything to send up to her except the usual yellow roses, but twenty instead of the customary twelve. He got them to send the bill to his firm. Then he went back to the hospital, discovering on the way that his hands had stopped trembling.

His evening meal, sandwiches, was on a table by his bed, the tea cold. A nurse asked him where he had been for so long. After he had eaten, he undressed and began reading a spy story, which was good and could be used.

Before he fell asleep, he thought again about Jenny's story and made up his mind that it was old-fashioned and unusable.

She kept appearing in his dreams, but constantly changing identity. She was a woman minister, then a psychiatrist who could see straight through him. But in between she was Jenny Holländer, standing in a prettily relaxed position on an empty floor, looking as if she was just about to dance.

4

There were a telephone and a radio in his room, but he did not use either of them. Instead of telephoning his authors, he dictated letters into a small tape recorder that lay on top of the bedcover. He tackled the spy story and it took the rest of the morning to edit it, divide it into eight installments, write the headings and résumés and suggest illustrations and captions. Finally, he thought up a title, one that was short enough and contained an attractive alliteration, but after lying thinking about it for a while he abandoned not only the title but also a number of the cuts he had made. He had lost the desire to leave his mark on other people's work (he had forgotten that the original idea for the spy story had been his own), just as he had lost the desire to telephone his authors.

It was the day after his visit to Jenny's; it went by very slowly. Though it was too soon to expect either any results from the examination or a visit from Dr. Ackermann, he began to watch the door and the doorknob with interest.

Early in the afternoon, Dr. Ackermann paid him a visit. During their conversation, he repeated the encouraging touch on Bruno's ankle through the thin bedcover. Ackermann's cheeks were red, as if after an extended period of time in sharp frost, and his handsome dark eyes were larger than ever. Today he appeared to Bruno even younger than a contemporary.

"Tomorrow we'll know if we have a tempest in a teapot or whether we'll have to rummage around in you a bit more," said the doctor.

The yellow pills had been taken away when Bruno had come into the hospital. He requested a couple more for the next twenty-four hours and received an unhesitating affirmative in reply. After Dr. Ackermann had gone, Bruno at first thought that he had misunderstood his position from the start. The likelihood of his being seriously ill was fairly small, and even if he were seriously ill, it did not mean that he was also likely to die, but just that he might have to undergo lengthy and fatiguing treatment.

Dr. Ackermann's visit half an hour later seemed peculiar to him in its very superfluity. Bruno had been given one of the yellow pills, not two as he had requested, and it had had no noticeable effect. He began to worry without any clear reason for worrying, and for the first time he had to stop himself from fingering the bandage on his neck, which was still a little tender. Another half hour later, he seemed to have abundant cause for worry. A technician appeared and took new blood samples, again sufficient to fill several test tubes. She did not know what the new blood tests were for. She had hardly left, when his room was filled with an unusually large group of doctors making the evening round. With Dr. Ackermann were several older men. Their backs to Bruno, they studied his case sheet, which lay open on the table he ate at when he was not in bed. The men glanced briefly at Bruno and at the chart behind his bed, and then at the case sheet again. Dr. Ackermann smiled encouragingly. One of the men caught sight of Bruno's miniature tape recorder and asked a few technical questions. Then they all left, and Bruno lay there looking over at his case sheet, which they had left behind.

Nothing could have been easier than to have got out of bed and gone over to read it. Naturally there was a risk that they might discover they had forgotten it, come back to get it and find him reading it. But the other risk was far greater. Bruno took neither the second batch of blood tests nor the overlarge group making the evening round (with experts called in, which could not be misunderstood) as a good sign. Supposing he understood his case? Supposing he understood it and understood that his situation was as serious as it could be?

The open, forgotten case sheet, and the patient lying peering at it—it was a story situation. Bruno had an author who was in the middle of a doctor novel and he could not help thinking about phoning him and suggesting such a scene as he found himself in at that moment. He pushed the idea away and gazed hypnotically at his case sheet. Did the fact that he didn't go and look imply something decisive about him? Did it make him different from all the others, or did it make him just the same as most people?

Someone came running along the corridor and he drew a deep breath, perhaps of relief. No one knocked; the door was simply opened, with such violence that it hit the door stop, swung back and slammed shut. A nurse with a red face grabbed the case sheet, closed it hurriedly, turned around breathlessly and said to Bruno quite unnecessarily:

"We forgot your case sheet."

Before his evening meal, he forced himself to get up and go out for a short walk. He was wearing his own clothes, while most of the patients walking around the tall building and the pavilions at this time of day were wearing red or blue

29

striped hospital pajamas with quite elegant black hospital robes. At a stall, he bought the weeklies of the competition—it was the day the weeklies were out, he'd suddenly remembered—and two yellow tulips to brighten his room. It was five o'clock and had long since grown dark. He noticed the temperature had risen and would be approaching the freezing point—or melting point. The low cloud ceiling caught the red glare of the city's night lights. He heard the stream of home-going traffic out on the boulevard; they were beginning to honk to get away from the traffic jams they themselves were causing.

His evening meal was there when he returned to his room. Together with the food was a vial of pills. He let the vitamins lie for the time being and washed down the single yellow pill with a cup of tea, which tasted of nothing whatsoever.

A little while later, he took the vitamins and ate sandwiches as he leafed through the rival magazines. It was half past five and he had no idea how he would get through the rest of the evening.

He began again on the magazines and this time read one slowly and carefully right through.

Next morning, he repeated his request for two of the yellow pills. The nurse returned with the extra pill after a conference with her supervisor. Later that morning, someone knocked on the door in a different way from that of the nurse and the porters, and he had time to call "Come in" before Dr. Ackermann appeared. It was Saturday the twenty-sixth of January, 1973.

"At last I've something to tell you," said Dr. Ackermann. He pulled a chair up to the bed, sat down, jerked himself slightly forward onto the edge of the chair and clasped his hands as if in prayer, before placing them one on each knee.

"It's not cheerful news," he said. And after a pause: "There are many ways of telling bad news. I imagine you're a man who would like to do without the fancy wrappings. It's not cheerful. You're seriously ill."

Bruno's first reaction was to ask for more of the yellow pills, but what he heard himself reply was not about pills.

"Seriously ill," he said. "What does 'seriously' mean? How bad does 'seriously' mean?"

He could not believe that anyone ever told a patient that he was going to die. He had never believed that the word "die" was ever "seriously" used to a patient. He had thought, and had perhaps also hoped, that Ackermann was a doctor who took the sting out of the truth, or even never told it.

Dr. Ackermann pondered for a while, and naturally even that was a bad sign.

"You have cancer," he said at last. "The little cyst we got out of your neck has proved to be malignant. It's a comparatively rare form of cancer."

"But it has been removed?"

"It has been removed. But your blood tests show that it's spreading. We examined your liver at the same time we did that small operation on your neck, you see. You probably noticed the small bandage below your chest. The examination shows that unfortunately your liver has already been affected."

The bed began to sway. Bruno tried to sit up straighter but suddenly had no strength to do so, either in his back or in his arms.

"Does that mean an operation or radium treatment or both?" he heard himself ask, unexpectedly clearly and matter-of-factly, as if they were discussing a relative and not himself. Dr. Ackermann clasped his hands, bent them silently backward and pondered for a moment.

"Presumably you are wondering why I've told you the blunt truth. It is against our usual practice. I have taken two things

31

into consideration. One is that I think you have the nerves and the intelligence to tolerate more of the truth than most people. Another is something I'll be coming to in a moment, an offer I am able to make you which means that you should know your present situation."

He hesitated. His voice seemed to come from a long distance away, perhaps from out in the hall, through a door, or through several doors.

"Naturally you don't feel up to much at this moment," Ackermann said in a different tone of voice. He produced a hypodermic syringe. "May I give you something that will calm you down a little?" Bruno nodded, and a moment later received an injection in his thigh. He lay waiting for it to take effect.

"Generally," said Dr. Ackermann, "generally, I tell a patient that he is sick and the treatment will be lengthy, but there are good prospects of his recovery. Often that's the simple truth, and under any circumstances, we doctors need the patient's will to live. One can die of the belief that one is going to die. There is no definite prognosis for cancer. Your prognosis is not definite either. But it is, nonetheless, as definite as it can be."

"And I'm going to die?"

The injection was already beginning to work. Bruno had a strange feeling that he was being transformed from the first person to the third, a person he could look at or read about. He had the strength to sit himself up in bed a little and to raise his voice.

"Why are you telling me all this?"

"First, because I think you can take the truth. Secondly, because I have a suggestion to make to you which demands that you know the truth."

"A suggestion?"

32

"We can treat you according to the book. We can find out quite accurately how far your cancer has already spread. We can operate, we can give you radium treatment, and we can, as we always do, hope that in the meantime a new treatment will be discovered which will help you."

"Why are you telling me all this?"

"We can hope for recovery, for a miracle. Occasionally it happens. We can put our hopes in research, in the future. And perhaps . . . *perhaps* we can also offer recovery, the miracle, the future, a helping hand. But that needs your approval, which is why I'm making this exception from my usual practice and telling you the truth instead of censoring part of it."

Dr. Ackermann had got to his feet and bent over Bruno.

"Is the injection working a little?"

"Yes."

"We cannot cure you today. We can keep you alive for a certain period, but no more. Lie down in your bed and close your eyes if you want to. You won't fall asleep. The injection was only a tranquilizer.

"We can do much to spare you pain, and we can always hope for the miraculous cure and medical progress which suddenly give us new chances of treating you and curing you. But we can also attempt to do something more active. We can gamble, and there's a chance of our winning. If we didn't believe that, I wouldn't be standing here telling you as much as I've already told you."

The injection was taking full effect. Bruno relaxed and had to struggle slightly to stop his eyes from closing. The doctor's voice was friendly and encouraging. The voice was talking to him, but not really about him any longer.

"We can't expect to cure you today. But we're in the middle of incredible developments, and not least in your field;

with the type of cancer we have found in you, things are moving faster and faster. We can't expect to cure you today, but we can hope to cure you in fifteen or twenty years' time."

Bruno looked at the man bending over him. His eyes were large and wide open, his cheeks unnaturally red. Was the man insane? Had everything he had said hitherto been as insane as his last remark?

"But this isn't merely something we're hoping to be able to do. It's something we feel convinced about. We wish to cure you of your illness. We wish to do it in fifteen or twenty years' time, when we know that we can. Instead of letting you die slowly now. We wish to freeze you down. But the decision will naturally not depend on what we wish; the decision will depend on what *you* wish. We do not want you to decide now. You have a few days. You've had an injection now and in a short while you'll probably fall asleep. That's just as well, as naturally I've just given you a shock. Perhaps when you wake up, you will have forgotten some of what I've told you; that I don't know. All I want to tell you now is that we have a choice: we have two alternatives for you to choose from, and before you could choose, it was necessary that we told you the truth. You're not falling asleep, are you?"

Bruno shook his head slowly.

"Perhaps you've read about freezing people down. But I'm not certain if you realize how far we've got, right here. We wouldn't suggest it if we didn't believe in it. We wouldn't dream of suggesting it to patients whose prognosis gave us more hope. Neither would we dream of suggesting it in connection with diseases—certain types of cancer, for instance— that we're not absolutely certain of curing in fifteen to twenty years. You're not the first to be offered this treatment, or this chance, this respite, and you certainly won't be the last. You understand what I'm saying, don't you?"

Bruno nodded slowly. Who, he lay there thinking, who

34

were "we"? Were "we" the men who had taken part in the previous evening's round?

"I won't tire you any more now. The injection is working and you'll soon sleep. I wanted to avoid giving you a shock. I think you're a strong man, but even a strong man . . . Perhaps I should have told you this in a more roundabout way, but I can't really see how. The situation is also a new one for us medical men. When you're clear again, you'll have time to think about it all. I'll keep an eye on you. Later, I'll explain to you exactly what we'd do to you, both the purely medical side of the situation and the legal side, the practical side. You'll be allowed to make your own decision by yourself. There'll be no pressure put on you. I'll explain the alternatives to you again and you'll have time to think about it—a few days. And for the time being, I'll sit here by the window and wait for you to fall asleep."

"Freezing down?" said Bruno.

The doctor nodded and sat in the chair. It was a long way to the chair, too far for Bruno to hope that his voice would reach. He imagined himself placed in the middle of a block of ice, an old-fashioned block of ice of the kind they used to have delivered every day in his earliest childhood; sleepily he followed memories of the block being laid in the bottom of a wooden cupboard that stood in the cool larder; by evening, the block had melted and the water was emptied away, then the next morning another block came. Bruno looked past the smiling Dr. Ackermann at the tall building that spoiled his view. Where would they put him? Who would see to it that the ice didn't melt?

"Who . . . ?" began Bruno.

Dr. Ackermann came a little closer.

"Promise me . . ." said Bruno.

Then he gave in and slept.

5

The yellow tulips he had bought himself were standing by the window where Dr. Ackermann had been sitting. Dr. Ackermann was not there. It was Sunday and Bruno had only the vaguest memory of where Saturday had gone. He had waked up after the injection, had eaten his evening meal and had read one of the rival magazines. He remembered only very indistinctly what he had read: a man describing in detail that seemed highly improbable what he had experienced in Afghanistan. There had been a page on cars and motor racing, which had bored him, but he had read it to the end, and there had been a couple of pages on royalty, which he had also read. He had not been himself, and had fallen asleep without becoming himself again, without making any decisions about his situation, without making any attempt to contact Dr. Ackermann. Thus Saturday had gone by, the pills and injection working together, and he had slept without giving his peculiar situation a single thought. Perhaps, he thought, without hope, perhaps the whole thing had been a bad dream.

But on Sunday morning he was certain that it had not been a dream.

The tulips glowed in the window. Bruno had bought them for himself. No one else had sent him flowers and no one had phoned, for no one knew he was there. He had not told anyone about his illness, or the alternative, and this was the result. No one had missed him for these few days, but for how long was he indispensable? He could phone someone, tell about his situation. He picked up the receiver and then put it down again.

Bruno looked in the mirror. Apart from the classic who-am-I? question and the equally classic why-am-I-here?, there was now another: whom-do-I-tell? The answer was: no one. He thrust his face closer to the mirror and breathed against it so that he could no longer see himself; the heat and damp that misted the mirror came from a body that was still healthy and functioning perfectly. He made a small circular hole in the mist with his forefinger and was able to see his nose and upper lip. He splashed cold water over his face, then shaving lotion. It made no difference behind his forehead and eyes. He realized with surprising conviction that he would not have been capable of leaving the world, even temporarily, if he were healthy. Nor had he ever imagined it. People with new ideas, with fresher ideas, would take his place, and he would be missed for only a short time. He had achieved nothing that would be difficult to forget.

In his diary, Goethe had noted down something like: *"Dreiundzwanzig, und noch Nichts für die Unsterblichkeit getan."* Possibly Goethe had been a little older or perhaps a little younger than twenty-three. Anyway, he had been younger than Bruno. The thought of leaving nothing behind him must have been frightening. Bruno picked up the telephone receiver again, and again put it down.

38

Immortality did not worry him, but he thought again: If you live the six or nine or twelve months the doctors have given you, you could write a story about a man who is going to die. You could also try to write into the future that Dr. Ackermann has promised you; you could write an astonishing novel of the future about a man who, in a frozen state, lives into the future and astonishes the world. The idea was rather sensational, and it was unlikely that any weekly magazine would publish it; but perhaps he would then have done something for his immortality? And what can you use your immortality for, he asked himself, when you are dead? You wouldn't even have any use for the money.

He got half dressed—that is, put on his overcoat—and went out to the telephone booth at the end of the hospital corridor. He found Ackermann, Josef Ackermann, but after the name was printed "Unlisted number." He stopped the nurse in the hallway and asked what Ackermann's number was. She did not know, or so she said, but she could ask the duty doctor, if there was anything important he wanted to say. Bruno went back to his room. He sat down in the chair and looked straight ahead, called a nurse and was allowed one yellow pill, asked for another and got it after some negotiations. His problems seemed less great; he received permission to go for a short walk, a walk to think things out.

A man who is going to die, who is given two alternatives: that he should live for a while and write his story; or die, wake up again and hope that there would be even better stories to be told. Should one live the time one is allowed and get a good story out of it? How, in all the merciless details, was the freezing process carried out, and then the thawing? Would not other people have been thawed out before him and already told the story better than he could hope to—one of his better

39

authors, and without his help, his helpful phone calls and letters?

The hospital chapel bell rang for morning services, the sound blending with band music from a nearby football field. Bruno splashed more water over his hair and face and felt sober, but not in a state to make any decisions. He pulled the bandage off and felt the incision. It was not unpleasantly tender. He explained to a nurse that he did not want any lunch and wished to take his usual walk around the shiplike building and all the pavilions. She put a fresh bandage on his neck. Then he left the hospital grounds and shortly after that found himself not far from the district where Jenny Holländer lived.

He did not know her well, nor did he know her any less well than he knew any of the people he had considered phoning. There was no one he could tell about his alternatives, not even her. But there was still some kind of relief in talking to a person who had her own problems, as he himself had problems—a mild way of putting it. He felt no desire to talk to a person who had no problems at all.

It was Sunday. Sunday the twenty-seventh of January, 1973. The streets were deserted and it was a gray day. He walked briskly, his whole organism still functioning perfectly. Only a slight tenderness under the bandage told him that he was not the physically fit person he had been before. He wondered whether the travel article on Afghanistan had been the pack of lies he had suspected. People finding themselves in the middle of a situation often judge it more subjectively than a skeptical reader accepts. Sometimes that subjective evaluation is the more interesting. Bruno knew that the experiences he was having just now could not be communicated. Were they more valuable, or less, than the well-considered accounts people produced when they could see the events at a distance?—accounts which, among other things, had undergone an editor's cool pen or direct censorship? For the first time in his life, he was not sure.

He did not think he could visit her on the pretext of collecting more facts for a serial that would never be written. Or could he? It was thawing and he could hear a couple of children skipping far down the street. The street appeared to be a long room as the gray clouds seemed to lower themselves like a ceiling between the two rows of facades.

She was at home. She let him in herself, and took him up to her light attic room.

"It was nice of you to come. I was just going to have some tea," she said.

"This time I've not come to pump you for information for a story. This time I've come just because I wanted to see you."

"It doesn't make any difference," she said. "At the most, I'm slightly more flattered. Not," she added, "not that I had anything against your pumping me for ideas the other day."

She was wearing black slacks and a black sweater. She had prominent cheekbones and a large mouth with a lot of perfect white teeth. She still smelled of soap, but not, this time, of sweat. He realized that he was a little in love with her, or at least felt strongly attracted to her. Over the tea, she said:

"You want to tell me something, don't you?"

He shook his head and wished he could have nodded. In the mirror that covered the wall opposite the sofa they were sitting on, he saw himself shake his head and could not perceive from the outside of this head-shaking man that in reality he wanted to nod.

"I don't want to go on about it, but there *is* something worrying you."

"Yes," he said. "Perhaps. But it's nothing I can tell you about."

41

"Why not?"

She saw that he was studying himself in the mirror and caught his eye there, instead of directly.

"It's something I have to find my way out of myself. While I am finding my way out, you help me by letting me sit here drinking tea."

Were they magazine sentences? Were they the banal remarks with which he would have filled his die-or-be-frozendown novel? Anyway, now they were things he had actually said to her, and not just something he had sat and thought about.

"I envy you," he said. "You have your ballet and you live for it, don't you? Tell me, do you live for *anything* else?"

She shook her head, smiling. "No, not really."

"A little love?"

"Sometimes. Perhaps only something like it."

She seemed embarrassed by what she had said and busied herself lighting the two candles on the table. There were church bells nearby, the sound of Sunday in the empty streets.

"What I do," she said, leaning back on the sofa and pulling her legs up under her, "is probably live from one day to the next. If I try to live any other way, I'm soon frightened. Perhaps one day I dance well, or reasonably, and that's a good day. Maybe you'd call me ambitious, but it's simply a standard to live by. In fact I've never danced *really* well, but if I do someday, it'll be noticed, and the next day be forgotten. You might say it's meaningless to dance well, but it's the only thing I want to do."

"Dance well—does that just mean dancing better than anyone else?"

"That too, but not only that. And now you might as well try to tell me what's troubling *you.*"

Bruno finished his tea, which was far too scented for his

taste, glanced at his face behind a candle in the mirror, and heard himself say something he had not planned to say even a second before he began saying it.

"You know that I don't write stories, I only edit them?"

"Yes."

"Just imagine that we're in the middle of one of those stories I edit. A gentleman and a lady on a sofa. They don't know each other especially well. There are candles and tea and one can hear church bells and it's Sunday afternoon. We have the mirror and the rail and this scented tea we're sitting here drinking, I think. There must be some details so that people can see for themselves, you see? So the question is, what is *happening?*"

"Happening?"

"The situation isn't all that involved. The man has a fairly definite question, a wish. But if one of my authors simply let him get on with it, then I would say: Stop! It's not as easy as that, I would say. There should—"

"It's not as easy as *what?*"

"—be a prologue. And a psychological one. The scene should be set before you can act it out. Ten or fifteen remarks work miracles, as long as they're the right ones. All that about candles and church bells is fine, but it's not enough. I want to postpone a definite remark for a certain time, ten lines perhaps, two or three hundred words, a thousand units."

"What remark?"

"The following remark: Would you consider going to bed with me now?"

She smiled and thought for a moment.

"Are we now in your story or are we in reality?"

"Well, what do you think?"

She fell silent, still smiling.

"People always beat around the bush," Bruno went on

quickly. "Never say what they mean. Approach by some back door or other so as not to lose face. Listen to this. I've got a remark that doesn't hit the nail bang on the head and that gives a possibility of some last-minute face-saving. Do you want to hear it?"

"Yes, please."

"The man finishes his tea, like this, takes a long preliminary run, ten seconds—we look at the time—then he looks the girl in the eye, smiles—it's the back door he can get out of again—and says the following: I've a very serious question to ask you."

"And what do I answer then?"

"You just reply: Yes, question mark."

"All right. Yes, question mark."

"And then I produce the serious question. I say: The question is, have you anything on underneath your sweater *at all?* Now you have to answer."

"Here or in the magazine?"

"Here, for instance. If the answer is no, then you can perhaps be content with shaking your head with a smile. Exactly that. Then I've got the courage to say the following, as I keep on remembering to smile. My next serious question, I say, is a continuation of the first, but hops over about ten intervening ones. Would you go to bed with me?"

"And where are we now? In the magazine or here?"

"Here. Now you are hesitating, and that's fine. I fill up the pause by saying: I'm not a ballet master, Jenny. Your career does not depend on it, so you can do it for enjoyment's sake if you like. Please note that I am using this opportunity to start using your Christian name."

"And then how do I reply?"

"I would very much like to know that too."

She had joined in the comedy. Suddenly he saw in her eyes how brutally, or so it seemed to him, she broke out of it.

44

"Is it always so involved for you to get to go to bed with a girl?" she asked.

"Not always. But today I'm confused and troubled. I'm sorry if I've been stupid."

"You haven't been in the slightest stupid. I think you should let the girl in your story reply: No, thank you, but perhaps another day, when we know each other a little better."

"I think so too. But what is *your* reply?"

"I hesitate becomingly, and then, as I avert my eyes a little, I reply: Yes, please."

"Because I'm not a ballet master?"

"Among other things, because you're not a ballet master."

Jenny took away the tea things, and made the sofa up with sheets, throwing the cover and cushions behind. She went out of the room and came back in a dressing gown, her clothes over her arm. She put the clothes down on a chair.

"*Need* I tell you what's worrying me?" he asked.

"No," she replied, loosening the belt of her dressing gown. "Only if you want to," she added. "But perhaps it'd make you happier?"

He lay down quietly beside her, fully clad. Her body was muscular, as one might expect. Her ribs showed very clearly beneath her breasts and her shoulder blades stood so far out from her back that he thought one could put a match or a box of matches between them. Perhaps she's the last girl I'll go to bed with, he thought. Perhaps, after all, he should live the time Dr. Ackermann had promised him, make love to this girl every day and write a novel, his only one, about a man who is condemned to die, and about his love for an ambitious and melancholy ballet dancer, who has her life ahead of her. He would have to insert a short scene in which he seduced her (or vice versa) to the sound of soft music and with many preliminaries. If someone else were to edit the story, the scene would come out or would be completely rewritten.

"Do you use anything?" he suddenly asked.

The question came so late, and they were both so breathless, that he did not catch whether she said yes or no or something else. And suddenly he was indifferent. Whatever he chose, Dr. Ackermann's offer or the respite he had, he would not be alive to hear or even see any child that might result—the only child he had in the world.

"I haven't taken anything," he said a little later, and he could not make out whether she had understood him.

For a while, perhaps for a couple of minutes only, there was no time to think or explain. It could be because of the injection or the yellow pills that he felt so drained and peaceful, though how much enjoyment she had had from those minutes he could not tell. He sat on the edge of the bed and looked at her pretty, trained body. They smoked the traditional cigarette and then she began to feel cold and put on her dressing gown.

When she had gone out to the bathroom, he pulled on his shorts and trousers, noticed that they had acquired a hospital-like smell, and stubbed out his cigarette, which he had not wanted but had felt was part of the scene.

She came back fully dressed and slowly drank the rest of her cold tea.

"There's something worrying you. Tell me about it," she said.

He hesitated too long. Suddenly he could see that despite everything, she was living in her own world, with her own problems. If he had replied very quickly she would perhaps have listened to him. Now he realized that she was slipping back into her own troubles, and he would only make things more difficult for her by telling her about his—his absurd alternatives.

"Thanks for everything," he said finally, and as soon as he had used the expression, it struck him as preposterously cold. "You've helped me," he said, and it was, he realized, a hopelessly sentimental remark from the novel he would never get written. In addition, it was probably untrue too; who had promised him that he would ever be able to write a novel? He had never even tried. At that moment, he suddenly knew that he *had* made his choice—his ridiculous choice between two ridiculous possibilities.

"Shall I be seeing you again?" she asked.

"Yes," he lied.

Down in the entrance, he kissed her on the mouth. A church bell was still ringing, the snow was melting and the narrow street was full of the smell of thaw. A gap appeared in the clouds and for a moment the sun fell on a building at the end of the street. He did not want to leave this street, which smelled so pleasantly of the first thaw of his childhood, but even though he walked slowly, with dragging steps, it came to an end.

On his way through the hospital grounds, he heard the band still playing in the football field. Dusk fell and never had this world, even when he was a child, seemed so lovely. He was alone, and there was no longer any reason to hold back the salt water that filled his eyes and made a blur of the hospital grounds.

His evening meal was on the table where his case sheet had lain that other time. He ate a couple of sandwiches and re-read the article on Afghanistan. He looked at himself in the mirror again, and again watched himself vanish as he breathed on the glass. Then he lay down in bed, having taken the single yellow pill, noticed no effect and studied the tall building that spoiled the view someone had once had from the bed. Where, I wonder, are they thinking of hiding me away? he asked himself. The telephone beside his bed did not ring, but suddenly he was scared that she or someone else might find his number. He pulled the plug out and let the magazine slip down the bedcover as he closed his eyes and opened them again. But now the salt water had formed a thick film and he could see nothing through his tired eyes; he was a child, he was frightened, and that was no longer anything he need feel ashamed of.

6

The night nurse glanced at the withered tulips and took them out. Bruno got up and washed himself perfunctorily at the sink. At half past six his breakfast came, and he made no attempt to eat it. At seven the morning newspaper arrived, with a seven-column headline on international disturbances, which he read and absorbed, but then almost immediately forgot. He passed some of the time by reading the comic strips and the satirical pieces on the back page. At half past eight the barber came, and he sent him on his way; it seemed unimportant whether he left this world with short or untrimmed hair. The cleaning woman came in and pushed a wet cloth around the floor. Someone opened a window and the room was filled with the smell of thaw. At nine o'clock Dr. Ackermann came, alone.

"I'm sorry about that heavy injection on Saturday," he said. "I very much wanted to avoid any kind of panic reaction." He glanced at the chart behind Bruno. "You haven't taken a tranquilizer this morning."

"Not yet."

"Had a bad weekend?"

"Yes. I tried to phone you yesterday. Why is your number unlisted?"

"I came in the afternoon, but then you'd gone for a walk. Apart from that, I very much wanted to give you time to think things out. You still have two more days, I hasten to add. I wouldn't dream of holding a gun at your head. Have you had time to think about it?"

Bruno hesitated. He really wanted to say yes, but finally he heard himself say, "Not enough."

"Naturally not. But I thought you'd like to hear a few more details, now that the worst shock is over and you're quite clear in the head. As I said, I'm sorry about that injection, but I think it was the best solution."

Bruno hesitated again. Dr. Ackermann gave him all the time he needed. Finally, Bruno said, "I've been thinking about something. You've chosen me to be the first to—"

"Not the *very* first."

That made Bruno stop, but again Dr. Ackermann waited for him to speak.

"You must have made decisions that were far more serious than mine," said Bruno at last. "Now, there's one thing I'd very much like to ask. Have you investigated my personal circumstances? Has it made any difference to you that I am an only child, that my parents are dead and that I'm a bachelor—in other words, have no children or other close relatives?"

Dr. Ackermann paused, then looked straight at Bruno and said, "Yes, that has something to do with it. Very soon in the future, we shall need quite new legislation. In your case, the legal consequences can be foreseen."

"To recapitulate," said Bruno, gripping one hand with the other to keep them both still, "there are no legal complications, or at worst they are of manageable proportions. My illness has been diagnosed unusually early. I am young and would have had every chance of living a long life, had I not been afflicted by a fatal disease. My physical resources are very good. The prospects of finding a cure for my illness in the not too distant future are promising. I am the patient you've been waiting for, so that you can carry out your experiment, isn't that true?"

"You make it sound wrong. The experiment is not mine, but the hospital's, and, in a somewhat wider perspective, medicine's. If I—if we believed there was a remote chance of curing you or keeping you alive any longer, then we should never have made you the offer."

"But if I should happen to believe that I can complete an important piece of work during the six to nine months I have left? Or if I'm more frightened of being frozen down than I am of dying?"

"Then you simply say no. The decision is yours and yours alone."

"Tell me how you freeze a person down and then thaw him out again. Tell me why you think you can cure me in fifteen to twenty years' time. Tell me about the legal and financial arrangements that you have to offer."

Dr. Ackermann sat down, offered cigarettes, lit both and talked to Bruno for an hour or so. Outside the window long icicles hung down, water dropping from their tips. The freezing-down process was naturally quite painless, he began, as it was preceded by a total anesthetic. It was a question of lowering the need for oxygen in the body, particularly the brain, as rapidly as possible. The exact temperature, especially at the start, would be regulated from hour to hour. It was necessary during the freezing process to introduce substances into the blood, and partly change it, to avoid crystallization and subsequent damage to the blood cells. Ackermann emphasized

51

that his account, to put it mildly, should be called a simplification. "Science has used the last five or ten years to develop the techniques I'm now telling you about. I'm not sure whether you would want or would even relish hearing all the details. But they have been used on other occasions, and with success, on animals, and more recently on humans too. We are gambling with you. But it's not entirely chance. And we have to be realistic and ask ourselves a question: what have we got to lose? It is not our intention that you should decide today. You must think further and decide for yourself what the right solution is for *you*. I shall be here in the hospital for the rest of the day. You'll be given my private number and you're welcome to phone me whenever you like, even if it's four o'clock in the morning, if there's anything more you would like to know. We realize that you find yourself in a unique and strained situation, and there's nothing we wouldn't do to help you make the right choice. Not the right choice for us, but for *you*."

Dr. Ackermann was gradually speaking faster and faster, like a machine gun. His eyes were large and dark and he had burning red patches on his cheeks. It occurred to Bruno that he seemed younger every time they talked to each other.

"And the legal consequences?"

"You will not die. Legally you will still be alive. That is a service I am not sure we can continue to offer everyone who is frozen down. But because you're one of the first, we have made sure that it is a service we can offer *you*."

"And that means what?"

"That any capital you have remains standing and earns dividends for an indefinite time. No death duties, no other expenses, except what it costs to store your possessions."

"My apartment can't remain in my name? I have practically no capital."

"If it stays in your name, where will the rent come from?"

52

Dr. Ackermann went on to the next point: "We're also willing to store your things at our expense."

Bruno noticed he was smiling. "I'm the ideal guinea pig, right? You'd do a lot to get me to say yes."

"Not at all. I cannot emphasize enough that we're leaving you completely free. We don't wish to put any pressure on you whatsoever. And now I think you should take one or perhaps two of those yellow pills and go back to bed and think coolly and calmly. I know very well that it's demanding a lot of a person in your position to remain cool and calm. I understand as well as anyone that it's not easy. But you have a couple of days left to think over our offer. And once again I would ask you to consider that your final decision has nothing to do with consideration for us. You must consider *no one* but yourself."

Ackermann left after making sure that Bruno was given an extra yellow pill. Bruno left the two pills untouched. He got dressed, walked through the hospital grounds and, when his legs would no longer carry him, collapsed into a taxi, which took him to the office. If he had thought of explaining to the others about the decision he had made, then his plan had been abandoned long before he walked through the lobby. He sat down at his desk and placed new drawings and illustrations in front of him in orderly heaps. The telephone rang, but he let it ring on. A novel about a man who has the choice between living for six months or letting himself be frozen down? Too unreal, too unlikely for a few more years, and—especially—too late. Tell someone? Here or privately? Naturally it said something about himself, something conclusive and negative, that there was not a single person he could tell. And it was too late to do anything about that. Jenny had been the nearest—Jenny, whom he hardly knew (was it just because of that that she had been the nearest possibility?)—and if he could not tell her, then he could tell no one. Dr. Ackermann would have to make the necessary arrangements—afterward.

He took another taxi to his apartment and now he regretted not having swallowed the two yellow pills, or at least brought them with him. His legs would no longer support him and he was forced to sit down. The record of *Famous Mad Scenes* was still on the phonograph. He looked around his apartment. Was there anything he ought to destroy? In a drawer in his bureau, right at the back, there were two bundles of personal letters, love letters he had received. He considered burning them and realized that that was superfluous, if not theatrical. For one reason or another, he felt it necessary that there should be some kind of order in his apartment, and he went around removing surface clutter. He opened the refrigerator and emptied it, closed it and threw the food that he would never cook into the rubbish chute. He put *Mad Scenes* back in its sleeve and returned it to its place in the rack. Then he could find nothing else to do. He stood by the window and saw that the thermometer registered two degrees above freezing. The room temperature on the indoor thermometer was sixty-eight degrees and he turned the heat down a little. He tapped on the barometer, which moved from Stormy to Fine in one single energetic jerk. Then there was absolutely nothing more he could find to do and he locked himself out of his apartment for the last time. Cancel the newspapers? It was hardly worth the trouble. No letters had come while he had been away. He put both apartment keys in the meter closet and took the elevator down.

Another taxi, this time back to the hospital. You can always change your mind, he thought, but the possibility was utterly theoretical. At the hospital, he asked to see Dr. Ackermann and got a secretary to call him from a meeting, which she said was very important.

54

"Anything new?"

"I've decided."

"Aren't we being a little hasty?"

"No. I want to be frozen down."

"Why not think it over for another day or two?"

"Try to put yourself in my position."

"That's not easy."

"I want to be frozen down, and it must be today."

"Impossible."

"Then tomorrow."

"There are papers to be filled out. The day after tomorrow is the earliest. And then you've a little more time to change your mind."

"Tomorrow."

"I'll see what I can do."

It was Monday the twenty-eighth of January, 1973. He went back to his room and took the two yellow pills that had been left for him. He had no appetite, and when he ate something anyway—it was five o'clock and his evening meal had been brought and looked rather special—he had to get rid of it again. The telephone did not ring and he did not use it himself. He put the radio into the bottom of the only closet in the room, so that he did not need to look at it. The magazines he crumpled up and threw into the wastebasket and then he placed the basket outside the door. Two pills did not help him sleep, nor did, later on, an injection. Through a ventilator came the smell of thaw, and the distant sounds of the city wafted in to him. Against all his expectations, he finally slept for an hour or two before the night nurse came in to put his washing things by the bed.

Then there was but little more. He washed and shaved thoroughly, was given two more yellow pills, lay down on his bedcover and studied the ceiling, rejected the morning papers

and the barber, and waited for the time to go by. At ten
o'clock, Dr. Ackermann and three men from Friday's evening
round came in. All four of them seemed more nervous than
he was, he thought.

He was given the papers and signed without reading them.
He allowed himself to be rolled into an operating room, the
four men keeping up with him. He was given an injection and
felt that all responsibility had been taken away from him and
that he did not have to think a single thought. His neck itched
a bit.

Ackermann bent over his bed when it had stopped moving.

"In one way I envy you. In twenty years you will still be
young, and I, at best, will be old. You're going to experience
something we others won't experience. You're going to experience something of the future, something we others will perhaps never experience."

And with utter absurdity, while Bruno nodded slowly to
stop him from saying any more, Dr. Ackermann said:

"Cheer up!"

Someone approached from behind and something was
quickly placed over Bruno's nose, something that smelled of
diving under water and not being able to come up again. Perhaps he had regrets, but now it was too late. Ackermann
smiled and went away. His whole body whirred and it was
not possible to breathe.

A picture: the pane of glass is covered with ice crystals and
you melt it with a coin that has lain on the radiator, and then
blow your warm breath at a small circular opening in the ice
crystals, which opens out only onto the winter's dark. Then on
top of the first picture comes another: an open hole in a frozen
lake. The hard sound of your skates and the terror of having
skated close to an open hole. Perhaps there are more holes and
now the thin ice is cracking. You realize that you are alone on

56

the lake and that for some reason or another you cannot make a single sound.

But then the second picture also vanishes and there are no more pictures, there is nothing more of anything. For one moment more, Bruno is Bruno, and then he is no longer. The pictures have gone and Bruno has gone, and there is no one left.

1995

7

He does not wake up during the course of a few hours. Nor during the course of a day, or a few days. The process takes at least a week, probably more. During all this time he is neither conscious nor unconscious, and that is related to a number of problems.

Someone shakes him. Someone bends over him. He does not know who he is, where he comes from or where he may be going. For a while, it seems to him that he is on his way out of a warm cave, which means shelter, out into a number of demands to open his eyes and receive impressions. A face glides right past his field of vision and somehow the vowel in the word "face" seems to penetrate. He cannot move his arms very much because something is fastened to them. In pain and discomfort, he is coming out of the warm, dark constriction which is his favorite place. Remarkable, because the opposite feeling, cold, also seems to be connected with the shelter he has hidden himself away in for so long. And here are two concepts (though still far from words): warmth and cold. He is cold. He whispers a word with a consonant at the beginning:

mother. Now mother has gone and he has to manage on his own. It is, actually, the same thing the many smiling (yes, a word connected with faces: smiling) faces tell him. But then they leave him to have a little peace and he is back in the warmth (or is it the cold? the two concepts melt together; warmth is perhaps to be allowed to be cold in peace).

Someone suggests that he keep his eyes open for a moment. Someone—who? A face. Someone pats his cheeks, and that he has felt before. Has he been away ten minutes? It feels like that, and it doesn't feel like that. He has certainly been away longer. He wants to be away longer still. And now they (who —they?) leave him in peace. He plops with profound satisfaction back into the cave; it is cold outside the cave, and hostile demands are made—demands that you should smile in return for their smiles.

Days and nights probably go by, but then they are there again. They force him to sit up. He is no longer tied with tubes by his wrists (one word—one syllable) and ankles (another word, another two syllables, one vowel). They support him and his legs move automatically. They place him in a bath (a new word, refound) and the warm water is a cave he creeps into, his knees up to his chin. He stands, wrapped in a large piece of toweling, and they hold him up, slapping his cheeks. The word "towel," with stress on the first syllable, resounds through him. He has a momentary feeling that he has been away for only a few days. They apparently understand the expression in his eyes and take him back to his bed. They demand nothing of him—no action, no words. He glides deeply down into himself.

A long time goes by. He is given another bath. The tube on his wrists is gone. He is lying on his back, studying the ceiling, thinking about his being alive. Says to the next face: *Alive!* The face goes away and he has been away, and cries: *Alive?*

The face is there again and it smiles and nods its head. He says: *Warmth.* The face turns negatively, he thinks, from side to side. Then he is alone again.

A cup with a spout approaches his face and by reflex action he opens his mouth to receive it, and sucks. Something sweet and heavy runs down into his mouth and throat. For the first time, he makes a calculation: a month has gone by, he has been . . . away a month. Or a year or longer. A longer time than he has ever been away before. He must know exactly how long, but for the time being there is no word which answers to the concept of time. Long, short. "Short" he rejects, "long" he wants to use, but he cannot say a sentence, and he is alone and there is no one to listen to the sentence he does not say. Then they persuade (anyway, tell) him again to creep down into the warm bath ("bath," a new, easy word; he repeats it, they smile affirmatively). They stick a hypodermic into him. He empties himself through openings in his body, one near his head (his mouth), and another farther away. Someone pushes something under him, makes him raise his body, makes him do it again. Again something is pushed in between his lips and taken out again. This time he keeps the liquid inside him.

Darkness, night. Day, light. He says: *Bruno.* And they smile enthusiastically. He says *time* or perhaps just a long *i,* and no one hears it. Another bath, more between his lips, darkness, light, darkness, light. *Bruno;* they nod. Other words—mostly vowels—their faces approaching his to catch what he says. *Bruno* is the key word every time. Enthusiasm every time.

Is it right that he is very happy (as against the opposite)? There is nothing that appears without its opposite. Vowels, consonants; warmth, cold. Dark, light. Happy, the opposite. Alive, the opposite. Mother, mother not there. Bath, no bath. A new word, very difficult, long and important, but they do not understand it: *Ackermann.* Faces, alone. Laughter, something that is not understood. Questions (words), words that do not make them nod.

Alone, in the dark, he finds his way to three tremendously complicated words: "Fiction," "Editor," "Editing." The last two are similar, the first different. To the faces that appear again, he says, already sure that it will not make them smile or nod: *Editing*, and then, in defiance: *Ackermann*. And: *Skates*. And finally: *Bruno*, which as usual produces a reaction.

In the warm, comforting bath, he follows with his fingers the outline of his body and discovers that he has two scars above his loins, scars which turn around his body's corners and almost touch each other. At this moment, he hardly knows either "loin" or "scar" and gives up asking a question, which soon after is forgotten. Wrapped in a towel, he supports himself against a tiled wall and says to someone that he is alive, he is living (two ways of saying the same thing), which is confirmed by one of those smiles he has got used to and which mean that real conversation, exchange of feelings and thoughts, is still considered impossible. He must wait patiently.

A curtain flaps away from the window, toward his bed. For a moment, the curtain reveals a window frame and blue sky, which makes his eyes fill with opaque fluid. When the fluid has gone, he sniffs in through his nose the smell of something familiar. The familiarity arouses him and to the next face that appears, he says: *Year*. And now at last there is communication. The face replies: *Nineteen hundred and ninety-five*. Although the figure means nothing to him, he can remember it. And later, when he is alone and still repeating it to himself, it begins to mean something; nineteenhundredandninetyfive. He does not understand it, but he understands that he will be able to use it later.

And he is right. After more dark, more light, more baths and more faces, he says slowly and calmly to himself: You must subtract something. And then again later: You must subtract seventy-three from ninety-five. That's . . . too involved. But again later: Twenty-two. And now he recognizes the faces and keeps them apart from one another. There are . . . men and there are women. There are several of each kind. The women hesitate the longest when he utters his words, and there are more of them (but they go in the end; he can't get any of them to stay long enough). *Twenty-two*, he says. And at once there is contact. A female face replies: *Twenty-two.* Bruno wants to say more, but there is no more they can agree on yet.

New words appear: *Well! Operated?* Headshake. *But well?* Nod. *Yes, well.* And . . . his fingers run around the incomprehensible scars; scars which just about reach clear around his loins. *Operation?* Headshake.

Well how? Bruno asks a man's face (anyway, they are the ones who know), and the reply comes in one word, which becomes meaningful a couple of hours later: *Medically.* Bruno is alone, looking up at the ceiling and repeating and repeating: Nineteen hundred and ninety-five. Twenty-two years. And then again later (but perhaps the same night?): I was thirty-two, I am fifty-four. Or am I still thirty-two? For the first time, he is overcome with anxiety and someone comes with a hypodermic. Later, he laughs until it hurts his chest, together with a large group of people who stand around his bed. The laughter is followed by sleep.

Yet another bath and suddenly he is clear in the head. *Where am I?* he asks. Either they answered him foolishly or the answer was too involved. In another darkness, he is lying in his bed and cannot sleep. He gets out onto the floor unaided, knocking something over, but nevertheless reaches the curtain, which blows into the room and brings in on the wind a soft and recognizable smell (and a number of weak sounds).

He pulls the curtain to one side and finds himself high up in a building, but there are other buildings around him that are higher. On the roof of one building he sees a row of lighted red letters, which he cannot combine into a word.

Later (but of course it is the same night), he again stands by the window and draws back the curtain. The letters on the nearest building gather up into a number of red words he can read: NATURAL LIFE. And on the line below, with green letters: NATURAL DEATH. Bruno turns his eyes to an even taller building, which stands a little farther away from him: ONE-LIFE CO. And even farther away: NOW-LIFE—MORTGAGES.

Or is he dreaming it all? He sleeps, wakes, sleeps, wakes, is in the bath. It is night again and he feels quite clear in the head. He discovers they have pinned a little buzzer to the pillow where his head rests and he presses it. A moment later a female face appears, a well-known one now. He is standing out of bed and he gets her to go with him to the window. But the illuminated letters have been extinguished, if they had ever been alight, and it is dawn. He thinks back with difficulty and asks her, joining the words with an effort but successfully into one long chain:

"What do those words mean? What does 'natural life' mean? What does 'one-life' mean?"

The woman draws the curtains across again and takes him back to the bed.

"That's nothing for you to worry about. You must just lie and rest and become yourself again, mustn't you?"

Next time he wakes, it is light and he again stands by the window. In the daylight it is not possible to discern the letters on the new building, which is higher than the one he is standing in. He can only see that there are letters on the tops of the buildings and he feels sure that he did not dream those remarkable words. But he cannot remember the words any

66

longer, or why it was so important for him to remember them. And next time it is dark, night, and he has a chance to stand by the window and look at the words, the curtains are drawn back but nevertheless he cannot see out. Why not? Because a blind has been pulled down (so perhaps it is only dark, not night?). The blind was not there before, he is certain: there is no cord to pull or knobs to turn to take a look out. He tries with his fingers to force the blind's slats apart, but the blind is not made like that, the slats (it is not a word he knows yet) are rigid.

"May I not look out?"

"It is night. You must go back to your bed and sleep."

In the daytime, the blind is up; at night, when the letters are lit up, it is down. Bruno knows they have put it there once when he was asleep. They have put it there so that he won't look at the strange words, which he has now forgotten, but which are lit up around him every single night; which he tries to remember and which fill him with anxiety.

8

One morning Bruno persuaded one of the doctors, one of the men in blue coats, to stay and sit talking by his bed.

The key word was "Ackermann." Bruno had two people's names in his head, Jenny Holländer's and Josef Ackermann's. He spoke the latter to the man in the blue coat and he made an effort to enunciate it very clearly. The man pulled the chair up closer to the bed.

"Doctor Ackermann," repeated Bruno, stubbornly and clearly, with equal weight on all five syllables. Suddenly the man's face lit up.

"Professor Ackermann," he said.

The other man had a small nameplate on his coat. DR. BERNARD, Bruno read.

"Do you know where you are now?" asked Dr. Bernard, with a wide grin.

Bruno shook his head.

"At the Josef Ackermann Center."

Bruno still had difficulty coordinating the facts he received and felt this needed more time than he was given. Dr. Ackermann had become Professor Ackermann, the whole building was called after him, and it was not a hospital but a center.

"I'd like to see Doctor Ackermann. Professor Ackermann."

Bruno wanted to see a face he knew. In his solitude, he had come to the conclusion that Dr. Ackermann must also be twenty-two years older, that his face could no longer be strikingly young and recognizable.

"That's not so easy," said Dr. Bernard, smiling. "Professor Ackermann is down."

"He's what?"

"He's down—frozen down."

Dr. Bernard motioned as if to get up, but Bruno grasped his arm.

"There's such a lot I want to ask about."

"Everyone who comes up has questions," said the doctor, sitting down again. "We prefer to answer them one at a time. It's unwise to try to make up for twenty-two years in a few days."

"May I, nevertheless, ask about three things?"

"All right. Three things."

"First: I am well?"

"You are cured altogether medically."

"Then why have I two scars?"

"That's a long story."

"Tell it."

"In 1982, we had a catastrophic kidney shortage."

"A *what?*"

"A kidney shortage, lack of kidneys in store—it was a spare part that at that time was still indispensable. A law, a law with retroactive effect, an emergency law, allowed us to borrow kidneys from patients who were down and had no use for their kidneys. We borrowed your kidneys."

"Did I get them back?"

"You got another pair when we found ourselves in the opposite situation—we had progressed to the synthetic computerized kidney and suddenly found ourselves with a kidney surplus."

"I got my own kidneys back again?"

"You were given a pair that were younger and better."

"But a pair of real human kidneys?"

"Yes. The law prescribes that if kidneys are borrowed from a patient who is down, then one has to fit the patient with organic kidneys again, if it is at all possible. Personally I'm against that law, because I think synthetic kidneys are superior in nearly every way, and I think that a patient who is to come up after more than ten years should have the best we can offer him. And now we've tackled far too much, which you will just lie there speculating about unnecessarily instead of gathering your strength."

"But you promised me three questions."

"You've already asked many more."

"One more question."

"All right."

"How old am I?"

Dr. Bernard was a small man with cropped hair. He had bushy eyebrows which almost grew together above his nose. To Bruno's surprise, he replied:

"How old do you think *I* am?"

Bruno thought about it. The question did not interest him. It occurred to him that he had still not reached the point at which the people who appeared in his field of vision were of interest to him apart from what they intended to do with him.

"Forty-five," he said at last.

"Very good. I am forty-five and I am fifty-five. We have a few people who have two ages. Biologically I am forty-five. Chronologically you should add ten years on, as I was down ten years with leukemia. We talk about biological age and chronological age. Chronologically you are fifty-four, biologically thirty-two. But your chronological age you can assuredly regard as a curiosity. You are thirty-two—period. And now you've asked so many questions, and I have allowed myself to be distracted into telling you so much, that I'm sure you'll want to lie here and speculate and get excited. So I'll give you a little pill which will help calm you down and relax."

"I don't want any pills. I've had far too many pills."

It ended in a dispute. Bruno fended off the glass and the pill so that water splashed over Dr. Bernard, who made an effort to keep smiling. Finally he went away and shortly afterward Bruno's meal appeared. They were still not giving him solid food, but the invalid cup had been exchanged for tubes containing a kind of paste or puree. The food made him so sleepy that he realized they had mixed a tranquilizer in it.

The nurses wore blue coveralls like the doctors, and they also had small pins with their names on them. Tight blue caps hid their hair. Beneath their coveralls they wore blue tights, which vanished down into long blue boots. Bruno was beginning to recognize their faces, separating one from another, although this was difficult since he could not see their hair. He studied their nameplates and tried to connect a feature of each face with a name. He began to ask them questions, but it was clear that they were not allowed to answer many of them.

"When will I be allowed out of this room?" Some time ago he had discovered, at night, or rather when the blind was down, that the door could be opened only from the outside.

"Have people got to Mars?" "Are weekly magazines still published?" "Is there a war on?" "How is it that I can see quite clearly without my glasses?"

The last question occupied him so much that he asked it again and again. He had been very nearsighted, and now he could see perfectly well without glasses. Each time he was given food, he lost the desire to ask questions. Even though he knew they slipped tranquilizers of some kind into his food, he was too hungry to leave it. He began to eat "solid" food—blocks of something soggy that could be broken up with a plastic spoon and that tasted faintly meatlike, but left an aftertaste that had nothing to do with meat. Other blocks had a more vegetable flavor, and again the same unrecognizable aftertaste. The blocks were brown and green and there were small hollows for them in the oval plate they were served on. Then there was a red block on the plate, slightly smaller than the others, and that tasted of fruit. In the middle of the plate were two cups, one containing something hot (yellow) and the other something cold (blue). The hot drink tasted like bouillon, with that same aftertaste again, and the other tasted sufficiently like beer that Bruno made up his mind it was simply that.

"Why can I see without glasses?" "What time of year is it?" "Why doesn't it ever rain in the daytime when I can see out?" (At night, when the blind was down, he thought he occasionally heard the sound of rain against the windowpane.) "How long am I going to have to stay here?" "What does 'natural life' mean?" "What is"—he had remembered the words again —"'now-life'?"

Obviously the nurse was not allowed to reply.

"Is this meat? Is this vegetable? What is it that gives an aftertaste?"

Some questions appeared to surprise them more than others; one day a nurse whose nameplate read YVONNE KLEIN said, "Is there an aftertaste?"

"Do you eat this stuff yourself?"

She nodded and took the tray away. But it could be the tranquilizer, he thought, that caused the aftertaste in his com-

73

pressed green and brown blocks with meat flavor and vegetable flavor.

Several doctors appeared to examine him, but most often it was Dr. Bernard.

"Three questions?" asked Bruno, trying to smile—it was a long time since he had eaten and he did not feel sleepy.

"One. One a day, and I don't promise to answer it. We've a long way to go yet."

"How is it that I can see without my glasses?"

"That's one of our minor miracles of 1995. No one need be nearsighted or farsighted or anything else these days."

"Contact lenses?"

"Better than that. We can make hardened lenses soft again and we don't even have to operate. Drugs have overtaken surgery and almost made it superfluous."

"Are you a physician?"

"Yes, you might say so."

"When will I get permission to leave this room?"

"One question a day. That was our little agreement, wasn't it?"

To the nurse, Yvonne Klein, who often seemed just about to answer his questions, he asked one that had nothing whatsoever to do with himself or his future.

"Tell me, are you red-haired? I think I can see from your complexion that you're red-haired."

She smiled hesitantly. Then she suddenly pulled her blue cap off and shook her head so that her long red hair framed her face; some of the hair fell in front of her mouth and she bit at it and caught it between her lips. Then she smiled again and pushed her hair back up onto the top of her head and tucked it away under the tight blue cap.

"What does 'now-life' mean?" Bruno asked, and he heard her close the door behind her.

74

In the daytime, he was allowed to walk around the room. It was large and light, without decorations or technical equipment of any kind that might attract his attention. There was a small grating in the ceiling and now and again there seemed to be a faint whistling sound coming from it. The only interesting thing in the room was the window. He stood there, looking out. The sun was always shining and there were never any clouds in the sky. There were tall gray buildings all around, and on their roofs were those letters that were lit up at night. Now that he could remember the words, he could also read them in the daylight. ONE-LIFE CO. NOW-LIFE. NATURAL LIFE—NATURAL DEATH.

Between the houses were streets and cars, but the streets looked empty. Was it Sunday? No; on the next day and the next day the streets were still empty. The cars were moving a long way off, looking rather small, and he could not see that they were very different from what they had been at the time when he himself had driven through the streets. The trees were of a light color that made him think it was May or June. He would very much have liked to throw open the window and smell the warm (he guessed) air, which was making the treetops move in the park at the foot of the building. But he had to be content with just looking.

The food still had an aftertaste, but it no longer made him sleepy. At night he had had menacing dreams several times, which he could not remember, but when he woke he still felt a slight aimless sense of anxiety. He lay listening anxiously to the faint hissing sound from the grating above his bed.

"Today's question: What goes on in that small grating above my bed?"

Dr. Bernard seemed to have more time on his hands than usual. He pulled a chair up to Bruno's bed.

"We're just checking to see that you're all right in here. We

75

take a look at you and listen to you. You're not feeling so good at the moment, are you?"

"No."

"That's nothing to worry about. We're gradually letting you off tranquilizers. You must see that being frozen down and then thawed out again is something of a shock. You've come through it a good deal better than many others."

"I'm not the first?"

"To be thawed out? To put it mildly, no. You're among the first we froze down, which means you've been down longer than most. But we have indeed had patients down and up again and then down and up again several more times, so even if you like to call yourself an old-timer, you're definitely not a sensational phenomenon of any kind. You're having an anxious time now, but you shouldn't let it frighten you. It's normal enough and you'll get through it. Shall we say you can have *two* questions per day from now on?"

Bruno reflected. Why was the sun *always* shining? What did "now-life" mean? Why was there so little traffic on the streets? What were all those tall buildings used for? Was the whole of the building he was in full of people who were down or on their way up? (He had made their new words his own—they were practical.) At last he said:

"What's going to happen to me?"

"Quietly and calmly you will get used to the life that is lived nowadays. We'll let you out into it slowly—for your own sake. Ten years ago, we let people free too soon and that ended in a lot of disasters. You'll have to go back to school for a while, so to speak. Believe me, we know what we're doing."

The sunshine. The doctor had gone and Bruno had been given permission to sit in a chair by the window, where the indefatigable sun poured in and warmed him. Yvonne Klein came with a real glass so that he could see the color of the liquid he was to drink and he let the sunlight play on it—it was beer, bubbles of carbon dioxide streaming in the sunlight up to the surface. Suddenly he knew what he was missing. Something to read.

"Have you got a book?" he asked her. She smilingly shook her head; there was, he felt, something intimate between them because he knew the color of her hair.

"May I look at your hair?"

She let him look. He felt attracted, not to her, but to the opposite sex. When she had gone, he suddenly felt restless. Now and again this feeling of restlessness became an indefinite anxiety about being alone. From now on, all his questions were concerned with getting something to read.

"Do books still exist?" he asked Dr. Bernard.

"Of course they do. But books are full of problems and would set your thoughts moving far too fast."

"My thoughts are already moving."

"I've another suggestion," said Dr. Bernard. "You'll soon be given books to read—old books. But what would you say to hearing some music this afternoon?"

Bruno lay down on his bed and waited. Long after Dr. Bernard had gone, there was a click in the grid above his bed and a moment later a voice said slowly and very clearly:

"*Johann Sebastian Bach. Air on a G String.*"

Then there was a pause, after which the music poured out through the grating.

Beyond the windowpane, the sky was blue and cloudless until the sun went down and the moon, a great red moon, rose in the light of dusk. Bruno lay outstretched on his bed, listening to Johann Sebastian Bach.

9

Bruno realized that fewer and fewer people were coming into his room. At first there had been many, but now there were only two—the doctor, Dr. Bernard, and the nurse, Yvonne Klein, who willingly showed him the red hair under her cap when he asked her to. It struck him that the cameras behind the grating, or whatever they were, easily were in a position to establish the fact that he was seeing her without the blue cap. They must regard this small intimacy as a link in his return to the world of the adjusted.

For a couple of days, Dr. Bernard did not put in an appearance and Bruno got to a stage of violent restlessness. Then there was a morning when Yvonne Klein left the door ajar. When she had served his breakfast, she said, quite unprovoked:

"Do you want to see my hair?"

He did indeed want to, and she pulled off her cap, her blue cap, and shook her head to make the curls frame her face. Could they see all this through their grid, and did they approve? The answer could only be yes.

"You've forgotten to close the door," he said to Yvonne.

"Yes, I have. Would you like to have a bath?"

He had not, if he remembered correctly, had a proper bath since that lengthy indistinct time when he had been waking up. They had bathed his body bit by bit for a long time.

"I certainly would."

So for the very first time during the long period that had elapsed since his awakening, he was taken out through the door, with Yvonne Klein's arm unnecessarily supporting him. In the bathroom, he turned his back on her and waited for her to go out, but she came toward him with soap and washcloth. Being away from his room filled him with anxiety, but the bath, the warm bath, closed around him like a tight soothing casing. When he got out of the bath, she again came up to him, holding a large bath towel, which she wrapped around him from his waist to his ankles. A little later he sat on the edge of the tub and let her rub him warm. Had they found through their grating and their seeing-and-hearing apparatus that it was this red-haired nurse who attracted him particularly? It seemed (he was not that light-headed) as if it was her assignment to look after him carefully.

She rubbed his neck, chest, his flat stomach (did one lose weight while frozen down?) and loins. Then she dried his feet and started thoroughly and unnecessarily drying him between his legs, and then she rubbed his penis until it stiffened—for the first time since heaven knows how long ago. Finally she put the towel down and matter-of-factly began massaging his penis with both hands until he had an erection, so that he really felt like a thirty-two-year-old, and an ejaculation—he did not feel shame at her witnessing it—a brief one, which, without looking at him, she gathered into the towel.

"Sorry," he said.

"Nothing to be sorry about," she said. "That was the point. Would you like to try with me?"

He heard himself ask a question that had never left his brain:

"Do you use anything?"

She locked the bathroom door and turned back to him.

"That's nothing to worry about," she said. "You've been sterilized."

"I've *what?*"

"There are too many people in the world. You've been sterilized just as everyone who is down has been sterilized. You're in need of sex and I'm here for that; apart from that, you mustn't believe that you are using me for something I myself don't want."

"Take your cap off."

She took off her cap and then all her blue clothes. The bath water was running out of the tub. There was a couch in the bathroom, presumably for physiotherapy, and when she had removed her blue uniform, her blue tights and boots, she also took off her underclothes and lay calmly waiting for him on the couch.

"Am I *sterile?*" His voice rose.

"The world is overpopulated. Too few people die and too many are still being born. Come and be a little nice to me."

Again she massaged his penis with skillful hands, until he had an erection. He was filled with rage over what they had done to him while he had been frozen down, but nevertheless he experienced a lengthy delight, associated with his own release and the study of her bright eyes and ardent breathing.

"Has Dr. Bernard decreed that I should have a little sex?" he asked afterward.

"Yes," she replied.

"Was it all caused by my wanting to see the color of your

hair, Yvonne?" he said, aware that he was using her name for the first time. "Do they keep an eye on me all the time?"

"Yes," she replied.

"And that's why you were the only one to bring my food after a while?"

"Yes."

He had become sweaty and was given another bath, a scalding hot one.

"Was I any good?"

"Better than most who have been down for twenty-two years."

"How old am I?"

"Thirty-two. The best age."

"Have you been down yourself?"

"Not yet."

"What does 'now-life' mean? What do 'natural life' and 'natural death' mean?"

"You'll be getting instruction in a few days."

On their way back along the hall, he saw two other patients for the first time. They were wearing blue robes and, under the robes, blue pajamas like his own.

"How long have they been down?"

"It varies a great deal. You'll be getting instruction together with some contemporaries in the course of the next few days."

She had pulled her blue cap tightly over her red hair before leaving the bathroom. Again he had to make an effort to see that she was a little different from the other girls in their blue uniforms and blue caps.

"Thanks for everything," he said to her, echoing something he had said a long time ago, when she left him to his lunch of brown, green and red compressed foods—but by now compressed so hard that the spoon would hardly break them. The aftertaste was still there.

Bruno lay down on his bed and listened to Bach, Mozart and Schubert. They did not allow him to listen to more modern music. He asked to hear some contemporary music, 1995 music, but Dr. Bernard just smiled. On the other side of the window, the sky was blue every day, and cloudless. They had abandoned the blind now, so at night Bruno could go over to the window and study the starless sky, the moon and the illuminated letters—NOW-LIFE, NATURAL LIFE—NATURAL DEATH, ONE-LIFE CO. One morning, Dr. Bernard thrust his arm under Bruno's and led him out of the room and down the hall.

For the first time, he saw the notice on the door of his own room, which he read before Dr. Bernard led him away: 1973–1995. BORN 1941. They reached a door on which it said: 20–25. Inside, there were fifteen to twenty people in blue hospital clothes like Bruno's. Dr. Bernard handed the rostrum over to a stranger who was dressed in green from top to toe, a man whose hair was not hidden, but shorn so that his red scalp was visible.

"We've been showing a certain degree of curiosity, haven't we now?" said the green man with ultra-short hair, "and that is quite natural. We have a right to have certain questions answered, don't we? and I shall do what I can. This is only the first of several meetings. I must ask you to have a certain amount of patience. All questions cannot be answered at once. I'd like to begin at the end.

"We write 1995. Many of you have been down for more than twenty years. The world has changed. We would not dream of letting you go out into it without preparation. A couple of you have already been up and down several times. You are fortunate. We've brought you up and cured you. In a couple of months, we can risk sending you out into the world called 1995. But rehabilitation or adjustment is necessary. Let me explain the 1995 situation to you."

Dr. Bernard and the green man exchanged a quick look. "We have had new probes out and we have very fine pictures of Mars and Venus. We've had and still have pioneers and pioneer civilization on the moon, but that's about the least important thing we've accomplished. Fortunately, we've discovered means by which atomic explosions can be neutralized before hand. We have had no war, no major war anyway. We have solved the world food problem by extracting edible materials from sea water. All of you have tasted them. We have overcome the problems of what were called unpredictable weather conditions. It rains at night and the sun shines in the daytime. For some of you, who have been up and down again, these are trivial matters. We have solved the population problem and found food of one sort or another for everyone. Just lately we have stopped working on these problems, because they are solved. The only problem of any size that remains is the problem of life. Man wants to live forever, and that is already as good as possible. If you are willing to pay the price, we can offer you a life that at the moment holds promise of lasting almost to eternity. If you wish for a life of so-called natural length, we can also offer you that. If you want to live forever, you have to pay for it in the form of hard work. If you are willing to make do with a life of so-called normal length, that too can be arranged, and there is no price to be paid. On the contrary, that is paid for. We have a concept, for which we have an expression that I personally detest, called 'natural life.' Eternal life is for me just as natural. But if you renounce an extended life, decalcification at regular intervals, transplantation of new organs, freezing down or periods of hibernation, then you can live without working. You can mortgage your organs and live off loans until so-called natural death occurs. If you decide on a so-called natural death, then no one demands of you that you shall lift so much as a finger. I can

84

no longer remember whether I am repeating myself, but in our 1995 society, we have reached the stage of a new class division. Society consists of two classes: the now-life class, which accepts death when the first organ gives out; and the immortal class, which works and pays for their—and here the sloganmakers have in my opinion created a word which despite everything still promises too much—so-called immortality. Organs and freezing down and hibernation as well, for that matter, cost money. The immortals have to pay for their immortality. They have to work to keep the system going and assure their privileges. For a large number of you, this is an almost incomprehensible situation. We have ensured that you have time to face the situation and get used to it before making your choice."

The green man stopped and Bruno, like a schoolboy, held his finger up.

"Can't one live without a mortgage and still avoid being chopped up when the first organ gives out?"

"Only if one has decided on the so-called all-life, as opposed to now-life. Dead people belong to society, according to the law of 1982."

"Don't synthetic organs alter the whole situation as you have outlined it?"

The green man hesitated for a long time before he replied.

"Yes. To some extent."

"How about synthetic kidneys?"

"Kidneys are not the only spare parts. We're still quite a long way from creating a synthetic pituitary gland or a synthetic liver. We still need the now-life system. Apart from that, there remain a number of people who are more frightened than attracted by eternity. And the central nervous system, the spinal cord and backbone are still problems whose solution we cannot yet see."

85

"Are magazines still published and can people still read?" Bruno heard himself asking.

"Now-life people still read. And many all-life people too," said the green man quickly, as if he felt he had been sidetracked.

"How much time do we get to decide?" asked Bruno's neighbor, a tall, fair man, who appeared to be thirty, but might be chronologically fifty.

"All the time you need."

"How many people are frozen down at the moment?" asked a woman, who must have been biologically between forty and fifty.

"We haven't," replied the green man, after a revealing pause, "we simply haven't the figures."

"And if we're to live an all-life, then we also have to help support them?"

"Not at all. They've paid for their freezing down."

"Are all those tall buildings built for people who are frozen down?"

"Some of them."

The instruction had lasted forty-five minutes and appeared to leave everyone in doubt. On his way back along the hall, Bruno was accompanied by the tall, fair man who might be his own double age. The man whispered to him:

"Those who can afford it, those who have capital, they're only up half of the time. When they're down, they're not down, but just 'low.' They get bored and want to have their metabolism set down. They're low in the winter, or what's left of it after the weather regulation; they're low at night, and they're low when they find they're bored. Why do you think we were given that lecture? Because they want us to decide to be up and pay the price—work—for the others. There are far too many who are low or down and they want us to keep them alive or whatever you can call it. The whole thing's disintegrating."

"Disintegrating?"

"Have you seen how few cars there are on the streets? Why haven't we sent anyone to Mars or Venus? Why don't we have any wars? Everything that man told us about the food situation and the atom bomb and moon pioneers was all just lies. They've been so busy with their immortality that they haven't had time to work at anything else at all. The whole thing's disintegrating. And now they're going to produce synthetic spare organs and there'll be no use for now-life people any longer. And then there'll be a to-do, believe me."

Bruno lay down on his bed and could not remember half of what the green man had told them and what he himself had asked about. They had placed a book on the table by his bed, *Glimpses from the Beginnings of Railways,* and he felt stirred by this study of old locomotives in colored illustrations. Out of the small grid above his bed poured *Eine Kleine Nachtmusik* and suddenly *Lucia di Lammermoor's* long mad scene. His food still came in green, brown and red blocks, but now it was solid and had to be cut up into small pieces with a saw-edged plastic knife. The sky remained blue and cloudless and the sun shone all day long. The trees down in the park did not seem to have lost their first greenness, although many weeks must have gone by. Now and again there was a lecture with questions afterward, which left Bruno no wiser than he seemed to have been the first day.

"Are magazines still in existence?"

"Of course."

"May I see one of them?"

"I'm afraid it's too early."

Instead, Dr. Bernard found him *Eight Weeks in a Balloon,* which, with memories of childhood reading, gave Bruno two sleepless nights. But the book was pleasantly long and took a long time to read. After *Eight Weeks in a Balloon*, he was given *Journey to the Center of the Earth*, which made him even more sleepless.

Yvonne Klein made sure that he had his daily bath, massaged him, undressed in the steamy bathroom and let him make love to her on the massage couch. This soon grew monotonous and he had another attack of rage when he remembered that they had sterilized him and equipped him with someone else's kidneys. After his bath and sex, he lay on his bed listening to *The Four Seasons* as his eyes wandered from Botticelli's Venus—which they'd hung up one day when he was in his bath, perhaps with the absurd idea that it would remind him of Yvonne Klein—to the window, where the weather was always exactly the same as long as it was light. Dr. Ackermann —Professor Ackermann—was "down," and he had stopped asking for him. The next name that occupied him was Jenny Holländer. He had slept with her only once, but she was the last girl he had slept with in his old life. Her name was constantly intruding. He lay on top of his bed and looked up at the grating, which was filling his room with "Winter" (how he suddenly longed for snow!), and thought about Jenny Holländer, repeating her name, seeing her in front of him, dreaming about her at night in detail, and speculating over whether she was alive now: Jenny Holländer, whom he had known for four days and been to bed with on the day that had ended with him making the decision to be frozen down for twenty-two years. What had become of Jenny Holländer?

10

There was more than one season. The green trees grew dark green and dusty. The sun was lower in the sky and no longer set between two high buildings, but behind the more eastward of the two. His food was still compressed into oval shapes like cakes of soap, but it had become even more solid and he had got used to the aftertaste. He was allowed to take walks up and down the hall and carry on conversations with other patients in a sitting room in the middle of the corridor, furnished with potted palms and several easy chairs which would have seemed old-fashioned to Bruno in 1973. There was a small grating in the ceiling above the chairs, which occasionally hummed or emitted a clicking sound. Bruno carried on several conversations with the tall, fair man, whose name was Henry, and who spoke in whispers.

"'Semicoma' is the new watchword," whispered Henry, who seemed to receive information from the outer world. "They hibernate at night and on Sundays and in the winter, and when they're bored. Hibernation extends your span of life, but they've also found a whole lot of chemicals that make them live longer, if you can use that word—live. Decalcification doesn't really work, only on the arteries and blood vessels. They're senile, but they've got young bodies. Have you seen an old man yet? Or a child? No one has yet solved the problem called age, growing old. The cells themselves, the brain cells, grow older while the rest doesn't change."

There was a clicking in the grating above them and they hurriedly started talking about something else.

"There's nothing to say about the weather—it's always the same," said Henry.

That was not quite correct, though. The leaves on the trees grew dark green and then yellow, red and brown. For a few days you could see from the treetops that there was a high wind. Every night, it sounded as if it was raining. When Bruno stood by the window at night, he saw streams of water running down the windowpane.

One day, Bruno had a conversation with Dr. Bernard about his financial position and his future.

"Your furniture has been sold, according to retroactive laws of 1987. You've been more fortunate than some others, who have had to pay out every cent they possess and more to have permission to be down. Today the rule is that only indispensable people can be frozen down at official expense."

"Indispensable?"

"Only doctors and nurses, virtually. There's a constant shortage of both. Others wake up to find themselves almost hopelessly in debt. You were one of the first and society still regards you as a kind of guinea pig. You can expect a nice little sum."

"But am *I* indispensable?"

"Scientifically, you're interesting."

"But I know only about one thing. I have ideas for stories."

Dr. Bernard smiled and Bruno realized that he had said

something stupid. How could he be certain that his stories still interested people who read stories?

"Are there still magazines?" he asked, for the umpteenth time.

"Of course," said Dr. Bernard.

"Why am I not allowed to see a single one of them?"

"Patience. Patience."

Bruno began asking very concrete questions.

"Do cars still run on gasoline?"

"No, electricity."

"Is there still television?"

"Yes, and the picture is wall-size."

"Can I go and look at it?"

"Soon."

"How many great powers are there?"

"The question of life and death has become the only matter of importance."

"Are there underdeveloped countries?"

"Not from a food point of view."

"Overpopulation?"

"There are perhaps too many old people"—"old" sounded as if it were in quotation marks—"but old age is a disease, and we're getting better and better at curing it."

"Aren't any children born any more?"

"Only when necessary."

"So the average age has risen?"

"Yes, if you still cling to the concept of chronological age."

"Who decides where and when children shall be born?"

"Shall we call a halt for today?"

The man in the green coat spoke every day on the need for rehabilitation but not about what they were to be rehabilitated for. On the necessity of not asking too many questions at once. On preparing themselves for the choice between now-life and all-life.

"Can I go back to my old job someday?" Bruno asked Bernard.

"Why not? We still need good stories."

"Are people still interested in ballet?"

"Of course they are. Why do you ask?"

"Does the name Jenny Holländer mean anything to you?"

"Nothing whatsoever. Does she work here in the Ackermann Center?"

The leaves fell from the trees, but the sun still shone indefatigably, day after day.

"The whole thing's going to hell, and they daren't admit it to us," said Henry.

There was a whir in the grating above them.

"Does the name Jenny Holländer mean anything to you?" asked Bruno.

"The ballet dancer?"

"Yes."

"The one who did marvelously well and got a lot of prizes and got into the weekly magazines?"

"Yes," replied Bruno, hesitantly.

"I remember that," said Henry. "But then I had my stroke."

"Holländer," said Yvonne, in the bathroom. "She was prima ballerina and then something or other happened to her and everyone forgot about her. I saw her dance once or twice when I was a little girl, with my mother. I saw her dance Coppelia. I think she got a slipped disc and had to stop dancing. Anyhow, she disappeared. Why do you ask? Did you know her?"

"Yes," said Bruno.

"Well?"

"Yes."

Bruno met Henry in the lavatory. Both of them turned the

taps full on. Bruno glanced up at the grating and then saw in the mirror how Henry's mouth came a little closer to his own ear.

"The President is a doctor."

"The President?"

"And nearly all the ministers. Doctors and politicians are assured spare parts and decalcification and everything they can think of. Sick doctors are frozen down for nothing in public refrigeration units. All the others who are frozen down have to pay for it."

"Where do you get all this from?"

"I was out three years ago. For two weeks. I'm an electrical engineer. They immediately put me in the drafting room of a refrigeration works."

"What happened there, then?"

"It was a private drafting room. We made home freezers, for semicoma and for long-term periods. Families often prefer to have their kin who are low or down lying in the cellar. Then we sent a man to service it once a week and see that it was all O.K."

"But what about you yourself?"

"I couldn't cope. I went out on a couple of those service calls. Then my nerves got shot to pieces and I was sent to a psychiatrist. Half the doctors are psychiatrists, and there aren't enough of them, either. They're privileged people too and get frozen down on the state."

Through the noise of the two taps they heard a loud click in the ceiling grate.

"But what about you yourself?"

Before Henry had time to reply, the Fate Symphony thundered out through the grating with such power that it was impossible to hear what he was saying.

The man in the green coat, whose short hair and bloodshot

eyes made Bruno think of a colonel, gave them a brief survey of general technical and social development, the world situation, the new words in the language, and then plunged into another explanation of the expectation of life and the need to choose between subsidized now-life, and all-life, which could be lived only by dint of considerable deprivation.

"Reluctantly, we have to subsidize now-life people. They don't lift a finger and they live in a whirl of pleasure—as long as they are alive. The only condition is that they don't destroy any more of their vital organs than the one that gives up. If we discover that they drink, they have to come out of the now-life arrangement, as we have to be assured that they're not destroying their livers. Cannabis is allowed, spirits forbidden. Use of drugs is controlled, with consideration for their kidneys. We still have preparations that damage the kidneys, but they are reserved for the working all-life class. You may well remember, from your first chronological life period, concepts such as bohemians and bourgeoisie. Or 'hippies' and 'squares.' The now-life people are the hippies of today. Though we've gone away from the idea that they should sponge off society. On the contrary, we now think that the two groups complement each other and both are indispensable. But I must warn you about one significant point: we still need certain 'spare parts,' but development has not stopped. The value of spare parts is not increasing; it is decreasing. We are about to produce more and more spare parts synthetically, and gradually better ones than the so-called organic organs. The trade value of organic spare parts is falling and that's a future perspective that has to be taken into account. One day society will not favor the now-life class as it does today. That's a factor you should take into consideration before making your choice."

Bruno, who had been dozing because the man in the green

94

coat was inclined to say exactly the same thing in a number of different ways, woke up and raised his finger in the air.

"How do now-life people *live?*"

"They use euphoriants, drift around amusing themselves, read books, listen to music. Many of them have to have treatment from psychiatrists because they know they are going to die when they die."

"May I ask a personal question?"

"If *I* am a now-life man? You won't meet any now-life people in the Ackermann Center. As you see, I work. I have six or seven batches a day."

"Can one move from one class to another? From now-life to all-life?"

"Under certain circumstances. It's expensive, and naturally the later you decide on it, the dearer it is."

"Couldn't you get hold of a magazine for me?"

"Shouldn't we leave these more individual questions until later?"

But later the man in the green coat hurried away. Henry went with Bruno down the hall to the sitting room with its old-fashioned furniture and its grating in the ceiling.

"There's something crazy about the whole thing," said Henry. "Can't you *hear* it?"

Bruno had bad dreams at night and in the daytime he could not tear himself away from the window, where he studied the fading trees in the indefatigable sunlight. *Ludwig van Beethoven,* said the voice from the grid above his bed. *Symphony Number Nine in D Minor, opus 125.* There was no way of stopping the music. But in a pause between two movements, a bit of an old song rose in Bruno's mind: "You were made to go out and get her." The ventilator window was open and he inhaled the autumn air, overcome at first with sentimentality, and later, when it was dark and the roofs shone with their

95

slogans, with anxiety. That night, lying awake, he found a glass on his bedside table, picked it up and approached the window. Suddenly he flung the glass through the pane. The noise brought Yvonne Klein in and after a conference out in the hall, she gave him a tranquilizing injection.

When he awoke the next morning, a piece of transparent plastic was over the hole in the windowpane. Soon after, Dr. Bernard appeared.

"Perhaps we should try a slight change of air?"

That same afternoon, Bruno was led down the hall, fully dressed and with a small suitcase in each hand, to the elevator, the door of which a nurse unlocked. Then he was taken in a car that had no driver, nor did it appear to have an engine; it simply glided along almost silently, out of the city between the numerous tall buildings, along a virtually empty highway. The car deftly avoided all obstacles and followed the road's gentle curves automatically. A nurse sat on either side of Bruno.

By evening, he found himself in a building that was taller than any he had ever seen, its balconies facing the sea. Bruno had his own room, with its inescapable grid, but the balcony was not a real balcony, as the space above the railing was closed in with some material that looked like glass, but gave off no reflection whatsoever.

The room had two doors, one onto the balcony and one that led out into a long hallway, much like that in the Ackermann Center, which opened out into a lounge area in the middle, where again there was noticeably old-fashioned and comfortable furniture and a grid in the ceiling. A telephone stood on a table. Bruno tried lifting the receiver but there was no dial tone. Two telephone directories lay beside the telephone. Bruno picked up the first one, which went from A to K, took it into his room and out onto the balcony in the evening sun.

He looked under *H*: Holländer. There was only one name, *Holländer, Bruno,* no address, just a number with ten digits. He went back to the lounge and lifted the receiver, but again there was no dial tone. He had memorized the number and he repeated it to himself as he went back to his room. For his evening meal he was given the brown, green and red blocks on a plate, out on the balcony. Through the glass wall that was invisible because it reflected nothing, he could hear the sea, which sounded just as the sea had always sounded. There was a narrow, deserted sandy stretch between the sea and the building he had been installed in. He sat repeating the ten-digit number he had read in the directory, as he watched the sun sink down into the sea. On the way from the Ackermann Center, he had seen an endless suburb of tall build- ings and then autumn countryside which apparently differed in no way from that of his childhood.

The impressions of that hastily executed trip along deserted roads had been violent and he felt that he was just about to fall asleep. Perhaps they had again filled his food and drink with something that made him sleepy. He had nothing to write with, but before he abandoned himself to sleep, he scratched the ten telephone numerals with a fingernail on a piece of soap in his basin. For some time after the sun had set, the cloudless sky remained blood red; Bruno lay in his bed look- ing at it and listening to the waves, which had exactly the same rhythm, he discovered with pleasure, as the pulse in his body.

11

Bruno received a visit as he was eating his breakfast on the balcony behind the invisible pane. His visitor was an elderly man with white hair, who introduced himself as Dr. Cavalcanti. Bruno asked the doctor why they did not trust him with an ordinary balcony without a screen. Two grids above the nonreflecting glass wall ensured that he both heard the sea and perceived the smell of seaweed.

"You must know that they still think you may have suicidal tendencies—a craving to exterminate yourself. You've broken a window and they've found out that books and music from your own time or earlier disturb you. This window cannot be broken."

"Do you really believe I would harm myself?"

"No. Not just now. But we have certain regulations we have to keep to. After thawing out and the electric shocks that bring people back to life, we have often experienced depressions which we can't neglect."

"You seem old. Your hair is white. You're the first old person I've met in my new existence. Are all your organs organic —your own? Has no one tried to decalcify you?"

"I'm one of the few doctors who has stuck to the now-life program, without betraying my sense of responsibility. I am just old-fashioned and have a weakness for natural life and natural death. But that doesn't necessarily mean that I use euphoriants and stop doing anything sensible. We are a minority, but it's a minority they cannot do without."

"And in spite of that, you still want me to decide on the all-life group?"

"I want you to make up your own mind for yourself. For the time being, it's a matter of keeping you in good heart."

"But I'm depressed?"

"Naturally you're depressed. Now we're giving you a chance to enjoy the sea and the fresh air. Don't be angry with us because we've shut you in for a little longer."

Dr. Cavalcanti went into Bruno's room and when he returned, the nonreflecting glass pane had rolled down and Bruno could smell the sea and hear it far more clearly.

"Yes, now we're out in the country, and we can talk freely. What do you yourself feel is your greatest problem?"

"I lived my previous life on one simple talent. I had ideas that suited magazine stories—serials. I must get to know the world today. One can't have good ideas for stories without knowing the world one lives in, the world that wants to be entertained, and in which the ideas will ultimately be found. I naïvely assume that the world still *wants* to be entertained."

"Indeed it does."

"How old are you?"

"Chronologically and also biologically—for I have never been down—in my middle sixties."

"And you've never let them decalcify you?"

"No; I feel a special and possibly unnatural satisfaction in growing older."

"And you work and yet live a so-called now-life?"

"Yes. The thought of doing nothing frightens me."

"Could one write a story about you?"

"I doubt it. I'm not all that unusual."

"Could one write about a ballet dancer who damages her spine and has herself frozen down until she can have another one and dance again?"

"Freezing-down stories have had their day now, I'm afraid."

"Tell me, are you afraid of immortality?"

"Immortality is something of a fantasy. Let us talk of fifty or a hundred years. Provisionally, one is frozen down if one is determined not to die. And one has to pay in advance, giving up one's capital and dividends, and with that one's heirs. Unless society puts one in Category A—that is, among the wholly indispensable. Doctors and nurses. The rest must find guarantees. It is not free to be down."

"When may I see a magazine? Read a story that has been written today?"

"Soon."

"When may I go for a walk along the shore?"

"Tomorrow, if you would like to come with me."

Dr. Cavalcanti made sure that the nonreflecting glass was rolled up again before he left Bruno. Bruno stood with his hands against the glass and studied the view, a long bay with dunes and a sandy beach, and he saw that there were tall buildings like hotels out on both points. In the evening, his food was not brought to his room, but he was called to a dining room, where he shared a table with an elderly woman named Mrs. Bourcell. Mrs. Bourcell took several pills with her food and told Bruno that she was halfway through a decalcification cure; the cure apparently caused her to alternate between very excitable and very depressive stages. Again, Bruno enjoyed being with a person who was obviously older than himself. He told her his whole story over the meal, which consisted of the same brown, green and red blocks that he had been given at the Ackermann Center, but which here they had gone to the trouble of shaping into steaks, vegetables and fruit.

Mrs. Bourcell and her husband had both been in their middle fifties and strong and healthy, ten years ago, when they had looked into their finances and found that they could not both afford an all-life. Mr. Bourcell, who was a contractor, but on a small scale, had chosen now-life and nonetheless had put all his energies into his work and firm. Seven years later, his heart had given out. Mrs. Bourcell had offered to go over to now-life to finance a new one, but he had persuaded her against it.

"We loved each other as very few people love each other," said Mrs. Bourcell. "He sacrificed himself for me. We both knew that I was too old to get anything out of a conversion from all-life to now-life. You have the best chance, he said. It was as if he no longer had any desire for all-life. I tried to dissuade him from dying, but the doctors were on his side. They let him die and shortly afterward I received my first decalcification cure."

"Your first?"

"I get one every autumn. Right up until spring everything goes well, but the summer is hard to get through. Then in September I have the worn-out parts replaced if there are any that need changing, and later I rest here for a few weeks to be decalcified and get my strength back."

"What do you do for the rest of the year?"

"Welfare work. I can tell you"—Mrs. Bourcell lowered her voice—"I can tell you that there are still things called slums, for instance. All the money goes to freezing establishments, you see?"

Next day, Bruno walked arm in arm with Dr. Cavalcanti along the shore.

"Is it true they've solved the food-shortage problem?" asked Bruno.

He thought Cavalcanti shook his head of white hair. But Bruno did not receive a reply.

"And neutralized atomic weapons and stopped all wars?"

Dr. Cavalcanti pressed his arm carefully. "The life problem has superseded all others," he said. "Those problems are not solved, just forgotten."

"One can drive cars without drivers, control the weather and, or so I've heard, watch television that fills the whole wall," said Bruno. "That doesn't impress me. I had expected greater progress."

Cavalcanti stopped to skim a stone across the calm water.

"Money decides everything, and life has become the most important stock in trade," he replied. "The rest are bagatelles, which would undoubtedly have been solved already in your first chronological life period. The problem with automatic cars and wall-size television is that the need for both is minimal. The all-life class is too busy earning money for their all-life and their various freezing downs to be able to invest in such things. And the now-life people are only interested in euphoria and other means of forgetting that one day they will die. I myself belong to a minority; euphoria bores me, but the new things bore me even more. If I had to name one single real benefit, then it would be that we can now read about the weather the day before and not the day after. I'm not talking about the sunshine, only about the wind and the degree of humidity."

"May I read one single new magazine?" asked Bruno yet again.

"Soon. For the moment, if I were you, I'd be happy that one can get a flat stone to skim over the water."

Mrs. Bourcell was hardly recognizable from meal to meal. Her depression died away and she talked more and more eagerly. She really did look younger every day. Bruno listened to only about half of her voluble stream of words. He ate with appetite, and the food seemed almost like the food in his first life. And he found himself missing Henry, who had complained constantly, had seemed informed on the world far away from the tall buildings, the freezing-down and rehabilitation centers, and had spread a distrust of everything and everyone that now seemed encouraging to Bruno. Mrs. Bourcell appeared so exalted and inaccurate in her information that Bruno soon gave up asking her about the world she came from.

One day while washing, he saw that the telephone number he had scratched into his piece of soap had worn off. He ran out into the hall, found the telephone directory and this time made an even greater effort to memorize the number—a certain Bruno Holländer's number, down there without title or address—before going back to his room. This time he scratched the numerals with his nail not in the soap, but in the soft wallpaper.

The place had a library and the most interesting book Bruno could find was a history of early steamships, with many colored illustrations. He sat on his balcony, which was open now that they no longer thought he had suicidal tendencies, and read about steamships, a blanket over his knees. Occasionally Dr. Cavalcanti visited him there.

"Does the name Jenny Holländer mean anything to you?" Bruno asked.

"Quite a bit. She was a dancer and became very famous.

Then I believe she was taken ill and no one heard any more of her. Why?"

"I knew her once."

"And you'd like to meet her again?"

"Yes, but she's not in the telephone directory."

Mrs. Bourcell grew younger and more and more lively, and one day Bruno was alone at the dinner table. Next day, he again asked Dr. Cavalcanti:

"Have you *really* no desire to be younger?"

"No. It suits me to be the age I am. Mrs. Bourcell, with whom you shared a table, will probably come back again one day. We can only give temporary help; on the other hand, we can give that almost indefinitely, to whoever has capital or will work hard enough. It frightens me."

"But you work hard yourself."

"To pass the time."

"Tell me something else. Why the hell did they sterilize me?"

"They haven't really. Not permanently. You can't have children whenever you want to, but on application you can have a pill that will unsterilize you again for twenty-four hours. In that way, we have the birth rate under control and can ensure that it is the plus variations like you and me who propagate—when it suits them from a population-political point of view."

On Sunday, a tinny bell rang to call the patients to services. Bruno went to pass the time. A clergyman preached a special sermon for the many recently thawed out members of his congregation. God has, he said, extended man's life. Why? We do not know. Perhaps so that man can serve God longer on earth, before God finally calls us home to him in heaven. Should God one day choose to cease calling man home to heaven, well, that too will be his will—then man shall serve

105

God on earth until eternity. Bruno remembered the hymns and prayers of his childhood. The following day a military man in a green coat gave a lecture.

"Many of you have waked up to a new and frightening world. Believe me, it is a better world than the one you went to sleep in. There are no longer problems that cannot be solved. But the world you have waked into still makes demands. I know only too well that there are evil or sick or weak people among you who spread mistrust and anxiety. The only thing you need fear is anxiety itself. Or the fear of anxiety. Later on in the day, I shall be available for more individual questions."

After the lecture, Bruno went to see the man in the green coat and asked, "How can I learn to edit fiction material that will interest 1995?"

"Edit?"

"Make good stories better. Shorten, find résumés and illustrations, pass on ideas. What stories do people like nowadays?"

"The same kind as in your first life, I should say. Good stories are timeless, aren't they?"

"But I must know about the new world first."

"Get to know it. Give yourself time. I personally will find you the contacts that you need."

Another nurse came to see to Bruno's welfare occasionally in the steaming bathroom. The girl was called Margrethe Sundmann and she was in many ways like Yvonne Klein—plump and red-haired. They did not make love on a couch, but she rubbed him dry after his bath and skillfully massaged his penis until he had an ejaculation.

From time to time, Bruno studied the number he had scratched with his nail on the wall of his room, and which he had quickly learned by heart.

A younger man, the promised "contact," came and assured Bruno that stories, whatever medium they were used for, were as stories had always been.

"Wasn't there a story in your first life that was always successful, about a woman searching for her vanished, kidnapped, or what-have-you child? That story is still successful. I've taken the trouble to read your old magazine. In a few months' time, in six months, *you* can write that story, and it will be successful again."

"But I never wrote. I edited."

"Write it or edit it. There'll be a place for you again. The class of people who can afford to read stories has indeed grown smaller. But they still exist, and stories are still written for them."

Mrs. Bourcell returned; her decalcification had been carelessly done and she sat at his table with a distant look in her eyes. After the meal, Bruno went up to the telephone in the old-fashioned lounge, lifted the receiver and dialed the ten numerals that had been printed after the name Bruno Holländer. A young man's voice said: "Hello?" Bruno put the receiver down again. At mealtimes, he felt even more distant than his table companion, who had looked older when she had returned, but who appeared to be retrieving her youthfulness this time without it making her so excited and voluble.

"Depressed?" said Dr. Cavalcanti, during one of their walks along the seashore in the winter sunlight.

Bruno nodded.

"Miss Sundmann is looking after you?"

Bruno nodded again.

"Perhaps," said Dr. Cavalcanti, "perhaps we should try to find out what's happened to your ballet dancer. I understand that you only knew her for a few days. Could it be, however, that it is her you want in order to get past this dead spot?"

Bruno did not reply.

"Perhaps we should try to find her together," said Dr. Cavalcanti.

12

One frosty day with a high, clear sky, Bruno and Dr. Cavalcanti drove away from the rehabilitation sanatorium on the coast in one of the silent, driverless cars.

"How does it really work?" asked Bruno.

"Very simple electronics. From the knowledge you had when you went down, it shouldn't surprise you all that much. Electronics in your time was already less beset with faults than the human nervous system. Incidentally, these constructions haven't changed for the last ten years."

"Where are we going?"

"Bruno Holländer. There are no others under that name in the telephone directory. I've taken the liberty of calling him up and he apparently had no objection to our paying him a brief call. Fortunately he lives nearby here, along the coast."

"You know something I don't know?"

Dr. Cavalcanti did not reply at once.

"Have you thought about the fact that she is probably older than you, if we do ever find her?"

"Why is he called Bruno? Isn't that still an uncommon name?"

"Bruno? No, it's not that uncommon."

"Wouldn't it be better if you prepared me a little?"

"My dear friend, I don't know any more than you do."

Bruno could tell that Dr. Cavalcanti was lying to him, and he did not ask any more questions.

The car followed the curves of the coast road and increased and decreased speed according to the sparse traffic. Bruno noticed that there had again been something tranquilizing put into his food, and he sat back in his seat. Before the car had started, Dr. Cavalcanti had pushed a plastic-coated card into a slot in front of the seat, and later the car had turned off on its own from the broad coastal road and worked its way along a number of hairpin bends up to a plateau, where it stopped. A narrow path took the two men on foot to a Swiss chalet in a rock-strewn glade. The chalet was like a summerhouse from Bruno's first life and reminded him of the old-fashioned armchairs in the centers and rehabilitation sanatorium lounges. In this respect, development seemed not only to have not progressed, but even to have gone backward. He also thought during the walk about the fact that in his new life he had never seen a child and that he had not met anyone who might be called old except Dr. Cavalcanti and perhaps Mrs. Bourcell, who constantly seemed to change age. And he thought about one other thing: he had not had a single idea for a story since . . . Six months or so must have gone by, perhaps a little more, of his new life.

A dog, a golden retriever, came toward them. Just before they reached the house, a young man appeared in the doorway. Bruno at once had a feeling that he had seen the young man before, a *déjà vu*.

"Bruno," he said, introducing himself.

"Bruno," repeated the young man.

Dr. Cavalcanti put his arms around the shoulders of the two men and followed them into the chalet's dark living room.

"My friend here," said Cavalcanti, after all three of them had sat down on wicker chairs and the young man had poured a small glass of brandy for each, "my friend here is eager to trace a certain lady whose surname is the same as yours and about whom you could perhaps give us some information."

Bruno felt his suspicion confirmed. The two men had already spoken together lengthily on this matter and he was the only one who might have a surprise or two in store.

"I've been down for twenty-two years," said Bruno. "In my first biological life, I met a young ballet dancer called Jenny Holländer. Now I've become interested in knowing what happened to her during the years when I've been down."

The young man took a sip of his drink.

"She's my mother," he said.

He took another sip and added, "Not that I noticed that much."

"No?"

"Her so-called art interested her more than her child, who seemed to have been neither planned nor wanted."

"And where can I find her now? Why isn't her name in the telephone directory?"

"My highly esteemed mother is down. She succeeded in becoming a dancer of note. Then she injured her back, an incurable slipped disc, and she chose to be down until they could equip her with a new spine, which I personally doubt they'll ever be able to do. That she had brought a child into the world by chance was obviously neither here nor there."

"A whole new spine?" Bruno heard himself say.

"All for the sake of her art. True idealism or true egoism."

Bruno hesitated before asking his next question.

"So your name's Bruno?"

"Yes."

Dr. Cavalcanti interrupted them. "Transplantations of spinal columns or transplantations of single vertebrae should be possible within the foreseeable future. Twenty or thirty years."

"My exact age amounts to twenty-two."

"This gentleman is thirty-two," said Dr. Cavalcanti, when a very long pause occurred. "Thirty-two, purely biologically."

The young man put his glass down and began to laugh.

Cavalcanti took over as host and poured another drink for each of them. Bruno noticed that the brandy blended with the tranquilizer they had obviously mixed with his breakfast, and with the best will in the world he could think of nothing else to ask.

Finally Cavalcanti said conversationally, "You belong to the now-life group, I gather."

"One *has* to belong to one group or the other," replied the young man. "Yes—the now-life group, for lack of a better occupation."

"So you shouldn't really drink."

"No, I shouldn't really. Who knows, perhaps my mother will one day have a use for my liver."

"Theoretically, I could report you."

"Nearly everyone in now-life drinks now and again, and the machinery needed to keep an eye on them is so overloaded that even if you reported me, they'd never get me. Concede that the whole thing is collapsing."

Bruno cleared his throat. "Where . . . is your mother?"

"In the cellar of some great freezing establishment somewhere, may she rest in peace."

"Have you *seen* her?"

"Have I seen her?"

"Since . . . she was frozen down?"

"Why on earth should I have so much as glanced at a deep-frozen lady who is five years older than myself and is lying waiting for a new spine so that she can carry on her absurd capers or whatever it's called now? Are you really aware of what one looks like when one's down? Do you think one is something delectable to gaze at? Do you think one can just go and pay a call?"

"Could you possibly persuade yourself to . . . to speak of your mother, whom this gentleman knew, with a little . . . respect?"

Bruno glanced at Dr. Cavalcanti and thought he saw an implied sympathy between the two of them, despite the reproach.

"Whom this gentleman *knew,*" repeated the young man.

Dazedly Bruno put down his half-empty glass.

"What do you live on?" he asked.

"Now-life. I'm mortgaged up to the eyebrows. The moment the smallest organ goes *phut,* I've had it. Thank God, I mortgaged myself in time. For the last three or four years, the mortgage rates have slumped because they're producing this and that more cheaply synthetically. My compassion goes out to all those who are eighteen today—that's the deciding age—and who happen not to be tempted by an all-life, in which they have to slave from morning to night to finance their spare parts and what it costs to be kept below freezing."

There was a moment's silence and then Dr. Cavalcanti said:

"Where can this gentleman take a look at your mother?"

"I doubt if he can take a look. But the place is one of the cellars in the Ackermann Center."

"The Ackermann Center—that's where I've come from," said Bruno.

"Oh, yes," said the young man, ostentatiously hiding a yawn.

Bruno and Cavalcanti went back to the car. The dog followed them along the road for a while.

"An unpleasant young man. I'm afraid he's not untypical of his generation, and of a group which is probably on the increase. To some extent, I must confess that I can put myself in his position and understand something of the bitterness which unfortunately was heaped on you at this opportunity."

Cavalcanti pulled the punched card out of the slot in front of the seat, turned it over and pushed it back into the slot. Silently the car drove down the hairpin bends, and again the sea appeared before them.

"Would you like to see her?"

Bruno nodded slowly.

13

Next morning, Mrs. Bourcell did not come down for breakfast. Bruno looked at her table napkin and in his solitude read for the first time what was written on her medicine jar, after he had turned it halfway around. ETERNOL, it said on the label. The pills were green.

After a while, a nurse hurried into the room and took away the jar.

"Mrs. Bourcell isn't coming down this morning," the nurse said.

She did not come down later, and Bruno noticed that her place had not been set either. That afternoon in the lounge, a fellow patient told him that she was dead.

"Dead? What does one have to do nowadays in order to die?"

"Mrs. Bourcell took an overdose of pills. She must have smuggled an extra couple of pills away at each meal and kept them. She had half the night to die in. And they still can't rise to a new brain."

Bruno tried to remember her. She had had blue-white hair

and had appeared to be between fifty and sixty, but it was hard to determine, for the age reflected in her face and indicated in her way of speaking more quickly and more slowly had changed often. Bruno regretted not having asked her more questions.

"But why?"

His fellow patient shook his head. "Probably an accident. But can you tell me exactly what *you* live for?"

Bruno had no answer for him. At dinner, to his surprise, he found himself sharing a table with Dr. Cavalcanti.

"Would you like to see her?" asked the doctor with the white hair and the tired, friendly face.

"Who? Mrs. Bourcell?"

"No. Your little ballet dancer."

"What was in those pills? Why are they called Eternol?"

"You have to call them something. There was nothing to make Mrs. Bourcell believe that she could expect eternal life. Would you like to see Jenny Holländer?"

"But she's frozen down," said Bruno.

"Frozen down and no longer so young. If I were you, I'd look for a really young lady friend, start all over, as you call it, and look forward to a time when we find stuff, unlike Eternol, that is quite without side effects. But I think that you should see her with your own eyes—Jenny Holländer."

Bruno cut his synthetic steak up into small pieces. "I only knew her for a few days."

The doctor smiled. "But she called her son Bruno. See her and get it over and done with."

Bruno tried to change the subject.

"I've thought of starting to write my memoirs," he said. "I was, after all, one of the first they froze down, and I can't imagine that there are others who've been down longer, down very much longer, than I have. I've even thought of a title. How does 'Up and Down' sound to you?"

"Familiar. At least one book has been written with that title."

"If I had her waked up? Couldn't she live with that back injury?"

"We haven't gone so far yet that we ignore the express wishes of those who are frozen down, as long as those wishes are financially covered. Your little ballet dancer has paid for the time we calculate it will take after prognosis for us to transplant vertebrae."

"But she didn't know I was to be up by now."

"Well, I wonder if she did. My friend, look at her, get it out of your system, and find yourself a new friend."

"Can't I see just *one single one* of this year's magazines?"

"Soon. First I think we'll drive to the Ackermann Center and I'll show you your little friend, who chose to be down rather than . . . take care of the child she had named Bruno."

"How can one *see* someone who's frozen down?" Bruno heard himself ask.

"With a little time for preparation in the proper quarters, it's like pulling out a drawer. A drawer with a glass lid. It's a privilege, but it's a privilege I am offering you."

"And afterward?"

"Afterward you'll find a little friend who is up like yourself and who isn't going down for the time being."

After dinner, Bruno sat in one of the old-fashioned armchairs in the lounge, and looked around. He tried to remember Mrs. Bourcell, but could recall only the sound of her endless stream of words, her white hair, which was arranged with great care, and the dresses she wore in the evenings, which had usually seemed too young for her. He tried to get a conversation going with some of the others sitting in the armchairs, but they were as distant as himself and each one of them appeared to be absorbed in his own problems. He went back to his own room and absently read his illustrated book on steamships.

Late that night—he could not sleep—he stood in the doorway to the balcony and threw the book at the nonreflecting glass that separated him from the sea and the shore. The glass did not break, but the book split down the back.

Next day, Dr. Cavalcanti again took his breakfast with Bruno.

"We threw our book against the glass," said Cavalcanti, "and I gather that the book was more damaged than the glass. Shall we take a morning walk along the shore?"

Bruno and the doctor walked along the shore together, past the point and into another bay, where there were endless rows of tall buildings, just as in their own bay.

"The offer still holds good," said Cavalcanti. "We're going to the Ackermann Center to have a look at the lady, who will probably be a little blue about the cheeks. Afterward, we'll find us a little friend who is up and available. Is that agreed?"

"Are they burying Mrs. Bourcell?" asked Bruno.

"They'll divide her up into spare parts and the remains they'll bury in the ground and a speech will be made by a minister, just as in your first life."

"And what are you yourself expecting one day?"

"Exactly the same, apart from the fact that I'll leave this world *against* my will. Suicide automatically transfers people from all-life to now-life. But I am, as you know, in the now-life group and want to hold on to the bitter end, because I feel more comfortable that way. Apart from that, in the future we will make sure that Eternol tablets are distributed one at a time."

"Which is going to make suicide harder?"

"That's the idea. There's no place for suicide in the new class

118

division. If society considers you indispensable, then society will also ensure your all-life."

"But you're a doctor."

"Of course, but I belong to the old order, purely legally. Apart from that, I'm afraid that one day society will force me into all-life, against my will. Did you know that nearly half the population today are doctors or nurses? And that ninety percent, if not more, have bound themselves to all-life? Come; now I'll tell you one or two of the little secrets that one should know to get a flat stone to bounce more than once."

Bruno made another attempt to break the pane of glass, this time with the help of his bathroom tumbler. The tumbler broke and the pane in the balcony held. Next day, his breakfast again had an aftertaste and on his walk along the shore, he was handcuffed to Dr. Cavalcanti.

"I'm sorry about these dramatic safety regulations, but you probably realize yourself that you are off balance. This afternoon, we'll drive into town and take a look at your frozen-down friend."

The handcuffs were not unlocked on the journey into the city. In the winter sunlight, the Ackermann Center shone rose pink, its length again reminding Bruno of a ship, though its height was greater than that of any known ship. The elevator did not go up, but many floors down. An old song rose in Bruno's mind: "Take a sad song, and make it better. . . . You were made to go out and get her." They walked down long passages. Dr. Cavalcanti made him swallow a pill in a bathroom. Then Bruno could no longer stand up and had to allow himself to be more or less carried along by Cavalcanti and a nurse, his legs dragging behind him.

It was a green cellar room, and there was a chair he was to sit on as he waited, then more passages, and at the end of a passage, another green room with a chair. The wall was full of green drawers with numbers on them. One of the drawers was opened and there lay Jenny. First she was packed in some thick material like a mummy, material which tubes went in and out of, and then they unwound some of the material and he saw her face again, her dark hair (cut short), her high cheekbones, her broad mouth which had concealed her fine white teeth.

"We've thawed her out a little," said the nurse, "in honor of the occasion. In twenty years' time we can give her a fine new spine and she can dance again, or whatever else she wants to do then."

Jenny was looking a little older. Bruno imagined that this was not just from the years, but also from the child she had given birth to. A strong word made its way into his mind; he loved her, even now, and she was probably the only person he had ever loved. Dr. Cavalcanti's plan had gone awry, he thought, before noticing that he was about to faint and looking around for a chair to sit down on again; but there was no chair and he sat down on the floor, where he closed his eyes, heard a buzzing in his ears and unashamedly allowed himself to fade away. The drawer was still open when he came to; they had left him alone in the room for a moment. He bent over the drawer and pressed a kiss against the glass that separated them. The glass was so cold that some of the skin from his lips was left on it.

The pain in his lips gradually went away on the journey home. Dr. Cavalcanti stopped the car by pulling out the card from the slot, and produced a lip salve. Bruno could remember neither walking from the Ackermann Center back to the car, nor the car journey out of the city. He was sleepy. Cavalcanti seemed depressed.

"Is it so serious, then?" asked Cavalcanti, without looking at Bruno. Bruno was too sleepy to nod.

"But you only knew her for three days. I've looked up your file."

That night Bruno got hold of the bedside table, tore it loose from the floor it was attached to, and lifted it up with both arms. He had already opened the balcony door. He ran right across the room out onto the balcony and hurled the table against the nonreflecting pane. At last he was successful. The glass shattered and he heard the sound of the waves, the same rhythm as the pulse in his body, and he drew the smell of seaweed and salt water deep down into his lungs. But the noise of breaking glass had been penetrating and as he was still standing there, listening and inhaling, they hurried into his room. They tied him down to the bed and gave him an injection. The next day, without Dr. Cavalcanti as escort, they drove him back to the Ackermann Center, and this time he was given a room without any windows. There was a grid above his bed and for sixteen hours at a stretch the light was on in his room. For the last eight hours, he lay there in the dark, and some ingredient in the food they gave him before they put out the lights made him sleep those eight dark hours without dreaming or wishing that the room had a window that he could cross over to, to study the tall buildings round the Ackermann Center and the illuminated letters on their roofs.

14

Dr. Bernard appeared again.

"And what can we do for you now?"

Bruno thought. It was a clear morning; morning as far as he could judge, as the light had just been switched on.

"You could freeze me down again."

"Impossible. Don't you understand yet that you're an old-timer? The eyes of the world are on you because you're one of our earliest successful patients."

"You could divide me up into so many spare parts."

"Do you realize that it's spring? Time for love?"

"You could freeze me down and thaw me out again when a certain lady is ready for thawing out."

"Miss Holländer?"

"Yes."

"But that could be twenty or fifty years."

"I can't see much of the spring. What about a window, which at least I could look out of during the day?"

"Unfortunately you have a tiresome habit of breaking glass."

"How old do you think I'll be in fifty years?"

"We've some fine preparations."

"Eternol?"

"Among others. We have more. Do you know what you need? A nice hot bath."

Bruno was given his bath. Afterward, Yvonne Klein dried him with a warm towel. He pushed her away when she began to massage his penis.

"Can't we cooperate any longer?" asked Dr. Bernard.

"No."

"We have a man who specializes in magazine fiction, who would very much like to have a chat with you. He's out in the hall, actually."

"Tell him to take a running jump at himself."

"The law forbids us to get Miss Holländer up. We haven't got a new spine for her, and her last wish was to be able to dance."

"Then freeze me down until she can dance again."

"We have other obliging ladies besides Miss Klein. Would you like to meet one of the others?"

"No. Tell me why you want me to stay up at any price."

"Because you've been down longer than most and we don't like sending people up and down all the time. We can't let ourselves be dictated to by some little crisis of mood or other. Also because you're physically in excellent shape and you owe society some kind of return. Finally, because you've been down so long that we necessarily have to regard you as a guinea pig and want to try to find out about the depressions that make it so damned difficult to get old-timers back into the mood again. You simply mustn't disappoint us now."

"Me disappoint you?"

"You've received an all-life without paying a cent for it. Others have to work all their lives for that."

Bruno's food was again in the shape of brown, green and

red compressed blocks. They had not given him a watch and his only measure of time was the light that was switched off and on. The door could be opened only from the outside and they no longer allowed him to be taken out into the hall or to listen to the military-green-clad man's optimistic and somewhat vague lectures. One day he kept his plastic knife and no one noticed. After lights out, he tried to saw at his wrist, but the knife could achieve no more than leaving a red mark across it. Dr. Bernard saw the mark the next day. After that, Bruno received his food in softer blocks and had only one spoon to eat them with. They gave him no more books, but occasionally he was allowed to listen to music through the grid above his bed.

Johannes Brahms, Violin Concerto in D Major, opus 77. Bruno stared at the grating, which was pouring out harmony. *Peter Ilich Tchaikovsky, The Nutcracker Suite.* There was no means by which he could get away from the music.

"Get a hold of yourself. For other people's sake, if not for your own. You don't own yourself any longer. Society owns you. Had it not been for society, you would not be lying here now."

"Exactly."

"Would you like to visit a publisher of magazines? Together with me?"

Something moved inside Bruno, but then he shook his head.

"Wake me up in fifty years' time," he said, and closed his eyes.

When Dr. Bernard had gone, he tried to stick the plastic spoon down his throat and make it suffocate him, but he coughed it up over and over again. One day, Dr. Bernard took him out into the hall, down along it and out onto a balcony.

"It's spring," he said. "Spring, and the world is full of stories to be told."

Bruno looked at the light-green trees down in the park and inhaled the smell of thaw and earth and light-green trees.

"Shall we go out into the city together and go into a publisher's? If I gave you a typewriter and paper now, would you like to write the story of a man who comes back into the world after twenty-two years?"

"That story's already been written."

"Whoever told you that?"

"I don't know my readers any more."

"Then write for yourself."

"I have never been able to write. You can't write without readers. And anyhow, I just *can't* write. My job was to have ideas and distribute them."

"But only as a start? A typewriter and a visit to a publisher's?"

Bruno stared out across the city and wished that there were one single cloud in the blue spring sky. He inhaled the air through his nostrils and noted the smell of leaves just out; he missed the smell of gasoline, which had been another constituent of the spring days of his youth on tours through the city. On a street below the Ackermann Center, he saw a strange scene.

"What's going on down there?"

A small group of people were barricading the street. Bruno could see some placards, but he could not read what was on them. There was little traffic, but after a while they managed to stop two cars.

"It looks like a demonstration," said Bruno. "Do you know what they're demonstrating against?"

"Childish nonsense."

"No; explain it to me. I can't get ideas for new stories if I don't know the world the stories happen in and that will read

126

them. Here are obviously other people besides myself who are dissatisfied."

"They're now-life people, of course. They're offended because the price of spare parts is falling, because we're producing better ones here. Synthetic ones."

"Why are they stopping cars?"

"They're doctors' cars. Only doctors have cars, doctors and politicians, and on Ackermann Boulevard there aren't many others besides doctors driving. Anyway, all our politicians are doctors of importance at the moment, and one can with some truth say that all doctors function as politicians."

"It's all disintegrating, isn't it?"

"Now-life is in the melting pot. We both know that there were also problems of adjustment and social unrest in your first biological life. That's nothing new."

A car with a revolving light appeared and a short while later the demonstrators moved on. Bruno saw them strolling on peacefully in a small group with their placards. They came toward the hospital and vanished behind a tall building.

"They're coming this way."

"But you can be *quite* sure that they won't get in."

"Are they Marxists?" asked Bruno. "Are Karl Marx's ideas still alive now?"

"Whether those young people in particular are Marxists, I couldn't tell you. There are so many trends—religions. Marx is still read and he still has his followers. Thoughts as simple as Karl Marx's might presumably be put into practice in any situation, and it is exactly that which reveals how worthless they are. Sound thinking on society ages naturally and dies when society changes as radically as our society has changed. Only useless banalities escape aging. Marxism's eternal attraction to the dissatisfied—and there'll always be dissatisfied people—is just the reason why it is inapplicable: its fantastic *inflexibility*."

"You've read Marx yourself?"

"Leafed through him. Read a little *about* him. There's no burning of books here, you know. The man isn't dangerous. We're not afraid of him. As far as your friend is concerned, your Jenny—"

Bruno let Marx be Marx and turned to Dr. Bernard.

"Bring her up and let us talk to each other. Just for ten minutes."

"We daren't. It doesn't do the organism any good to be frozen down and thawed out all the time."

"Can't I just go down into semicoma?"

"That doesn't solve any problems. We can only suspend or settle the age problem for those who are down. Those who are just low get older, although it is a slower process."

"They could decalcify me. What about Eternol?"

"It's a fiasco. We have been inclined to overestimate our capabilities. Eternol people also lose the will to live. Let us see you showing a little more will to live."

One day, Bruno stood on tiptoe on his bed and with his plate smashed the grating and something behind it. The music stopped in the middle of *Franz Schubert, music for the play* Rosamunde.

He had scarcely had time to stop the music, before they moved him into another room and began serving his meals in tubes again.

"*Isn't* there any modern music?"

Dr. Bernard no longer offered him visits to publishers, and the plan about the typewriter had also been abandoned.

"Couldn't I even see her once again?"

"For what purpose? We'll get you through this crisis."

Dr. Bernard no longer looked as if it was possible. The visits to the bathroom continued, but it was no longer Yvonne Klein who saw to it that he took his bath and there was no longer anyone to massage him dry with a large towel afterward. One morning—the light had been switched on—Dr. Bernard appeared again.

"Well, you're having it your own way. You're having another freezing. That's what you wanted, wasn't it?"

So Bruno's bed was put on wheels and rolled down the hall. Someone came up to him and gave him an injection. The injection worked swiftly and took away what he had still been able to retain of his anxiety. In a blue room, someone came up to him from behind and placed something damp over his nose and mouth.

The ice is much too thin to bear him. The ice is full of dark holes. It cracks and Bruno shouts soundlessly to no one for help. This time it goes swiftly and he is rid of himself almost at once.

2022

15

Chronologically Bruno was eighty-one, biologically at most thirty-three when they waked him from the world of the frozen for the second time. The thawing process went both more gently and more swiftly than the first time, if one was to keep to Bruno's sense of time, though it occurred to him that on the way there had been an episode, a brief experience of knowledge, that had intruded into the long (or short—his sense of time weakened) period of unconsciousness; an episode in which he had felt semiconscious and therefore in danger. The episode had passed, and it was not for the waking Bruno to determine whether it had not simply been part of the waking-up process.

Had he been up or at least "low" (the words were still not part of his semiconscious world) on the way? A face hovered in his field of vision, and it was familiar, more familiar (it occurred to him immediately) than anything from his other period of consciousness: Dr. Ackermann's face. And soon after that his reflexes arrived and corrected him: *Professor* Ackermann.

Professor Ackermann's face was young, with red cheeks and large lively eyes, as it had been the first time Bruno had seen him. Could it be right that it was even younger, more flushed and eager than the first time?

"Down?" said Bruno. And when soon afterward he was able to formulate a whole sentence (they must have got much better at bringing people up quickly), he said, "*You*'ve been down?"

"I was down when you came up. I came up the year after you went down again, or the next year."

"And now we're in . . . ?"

"Twenty twenty-two. Three twos. Easy to remember."

"How old are you and how old am I?"

"We have many ages. Every part has its age. Chronological age, biological age. Psychological age, physiological age. Average age, partial age."

"I've been down . . . how long? This time?"

"Twenty-seven years. All your vital spare parts are new or renovated. Can you remember your name?"

"Bruno."

"And surname?"

"Forgotten it."

"Job?"

"Forgotten. I think."

"Good. The cure has succeeded. We have a clean sheet— *tabula rasa*. We are thirty-three and shall begin a new life."

"While I was away I was suddenly"—Bruno hunted for the word—"*present* for a moment. For a certain period of time."

"That was almost certainly ten minutes ago. Memory plays certain tricks on us, especially with our sense of time."

"Jenny Holländer," said Bruno.

Ackermann looked troubled.

134

"You mention a name. A name of a person. What does that name mean to you?"

"We were to be wakened at the same time."

Ackermann frowned.

"Do you remember anything else? Say whatever occurs to you."

"Eternol. Lip salve. Mrs. Bourcell."

Ackermann spoke over his shoulder to someone else.

"Partial memory," he said. "We prescribe"—Bruno caught the word quite clearly—"continued Obliviol."

"Twenty twenty-two?"

Ackermann had gone.

"Twenty twenty-two. Two thousand and twenty-two. Or three?"

Ackermann was back again.

"Down all the time? Or just low?" asked Bruno.

"Down."

"But I remember something. It was nothing. And then there was something. And then there was nothing again."

"You were down all the time."

"And Jenny Holländer. Is she up?"

"She's on her way up now. We've done as you asked us."

"Lie," cried Bruno (but his voice sounded like a whisper).

"Truth," said Ackermann, and was gone.

Next time Bruno cried (whispered):

"Bernard. Cavalcanti. Bourcell. Jenny Holländer. Henry."

"Obliviol, double dose," said Ackermann's voice, over his shoulder.

Bruno was alone. His attention was attracted to something in his left armpit, an alien object. He tried to remove it but it was fastened, bound to his upper arm. He found himself in a room without windows. The light was on; both the ceiling and the wall were illuminated when other people were in the room.

135

The light vanished when they vanished. The alien object was colder than his body, but he could not dislodge it. The thing filled his armpit. When Ackermann had disappeared and with him the light in this windowless room, Bruno heard or felt a ticking in the object in his left armpit.

"The agreement," cried Bruno. "You're thinking of cheating me, aren't you?"

"Obliviol discontinued," said Ackermann. "Neutrol prescribed."

"Magazine," cried Bruno. "Fiction. Editor. Editing."

"Neutrol discontinued. Prescribe Memorol."

Ackermann had spoken and vanished. Out into the dark room, Bruno cried:

"Window!" And: "See out!"

The room was filled with light and Bruno thought: Ackermann will come in a little while. But the light disappeared and the next thing to happen was that someone came running, threw open a door, placed a candle on his table, lit it and ran out again. It was his chance to be rid of the object, and Bruno bent over the candle, became for the first time aware that he was naked, and tried to get his left elbow to arch over the flame to destroy the object. The flame went out and again he was lying in the dark. Ackermann appeared with a flashlight (memories of childhood, the summerhouse, a light under the covers to read by after saying good night), lit the candle again and placed it so far away from Bruno that even if he had gathered all his breath in his lungs, he would not have been able to blow it out. Bruno had realized that he was naked; now he realized that he could not get out of bed—he was tied to it; or something else had been done to him that meant he could move only slightly. There was a ticking in his left armpit, near his heart.

"Jenny Ackermann," he said next time it was light, and saw

someone smile. He hurriedly corrected himself: "Jenny Holländer." When it was dark again, the alien thing ticked violently and he came to terms with the dark and slept. Little by little, he also came to terms with the fact that the ticking in his armpit meant he had lost the initiative to call someone and cry out his memories, his name and the year to the faces that appeared when it grew light in the room.

One day he heard, half awake, a noise outside his room. Someone appeared and stood with both hands pressed against the door after having closed it and switched on a flashlight. The scene was mute, like a dream, and perhaps it *was* something Bruno had dreamed? The door was forced open by another person, in a yellow suit and with an instrument in his hands, who forced the first person to go away with him. The object in his armpit stopped ticking for a while and a number of names and pictures came into Bruno's mind. Afterward, someone again put a candle by Bruno's bed; and later the light in the ceiling came back and the candle by his bed was removed. Then Ackermann appeared.

"What's going on here?" asked Bruno.

"Nothing whatsoever."

"Guns," said Bruno, although the instrument he had seen was not like the guns he remembered from his youth. "Yellow man."

Ackermann smilingly shook his head; and now the candles no longer appeared. "Bad dreams, I expect," said Ackermann. It grew light when anyone wanted to talk to Bruno or look at him. And it usually grew dark when they left him again.

He became more and more aware of things.

"We're in 2022?"

"Yes. Three twos."

"How can I know that it's true? That I've not just been down a few months so that I'd be pacified?"

"Strictly speaking, you can't know anything. You must rely on me. You relied on me and I froze you down and saved your life. Now you must rely on me again. We write 2022, three twos."

"But I'm still only thirty-two?"

"Exactly. Or perhaps soon thirty-three."

"Can't I see Jenny Holländer soon? If we really write 2022 and if she's really on her way up?"

"Patience. There've been some slight irregularities in the organization of the work and we've got behind. We meant you to be brought up at exactly the same time."

"That's not true. You tried to get me to forget her and it didn't succeed."

"All right. We tried—for your own sake. But it went wrong and now we're sticking to the agreement."

"For my own sake?"

"Supposing it was a disappointment now. We try to avoid disappointments."

"But . . ."

Ackermann had gone, it grew dark, but later he appeared again.

"Does Jenny Holländer know of my wish to be thawed out when she could be cured?"

"She does."

"And what does she say to that?"

"She was pleased. Pleased and moved, I think. She said she had missed you."

"Moved? Missed?"

Bruno said the words out into the dark, for Ackermann had gone again and it was ticking softly in his armpit.

All in all, Bruno's second awakening went by painlessly. He had quickly regained his use of the necessary words, he could

138

remember much of what he wished to remember, and this time
he had Dr. Ackermann—Professor Ackermann—to refer to.

"Tell me what is fastened in my armpit."

"It's a small gadget that helps us to keep you in your best
form. Radio controlled. Better than pills or whatever they used
to use when you were last up and we tried to keep you under
control. Aid to self-help. It steers the organs and ensures that
you're in top form and in good heart. You've had Obliviol,
Memorol and Neutrol in waves. Much better than pills. Radio
controlled."

Ackermann could not be content with explaining anything
once. When he had explained something, he began again,
often using precisely the same phrases the second time.

"The agreement," said Bruno, interrupting him. "I was to
be wakened when Miss Holländer could have a new spine and
dance again."

"Exactly. Miss Holländer *has* got her new spine. We have
indeed wakened her. You will be the first to be allowed to see
her, when she's up again and you are yourself a little more.
Her new vertebrae *are* in place."

Bruno let Ackermann go and gave up trying to get rid of
the object under his arm. Every time the light went on, he
felt clearer in the head than ever and noticed more and more
that Ackermann seemed unclear in his speech. You are going
to see her again, he said to himself. We shall be up at the same
time this time. And in the dark, as the ticking continued violently in his armpit, an old refrain churned on: "Don't be
afraid . . . You were made to go out and get her." Chronologically he was eighty-one, biologically thirty-three. It was not
too late, he was still young: it could still happen. It was 2022;
but they were both young still, and they were to see each other.

16

At first Bruno thought that the nurse had been told not to answer him when he asked her questions. Then he realized, one day when two of them were making his bed together, that they were speaking a language he did not understand. He spoke to them from the chair he had been put in and discovered that not only did they not understand his language, but also that they overheard it as if they had long been used to some patients speaking a different language from their own, which they did not really listen to at all. Bruno did some calculations: the two girls looked young and must have been born after his second biological life period, if his judgment of age was still anything to go by. He tried some leading words with no effect at all—"all-life," "now-life." The girls finished making his bed with no reaction whatsoever to the words he had flung out at them.

Ackermann was in a position only to repeat what he had already said and Bruno asked to speak to Dr. Bernard, who by now almost certainly had another title.

"Low," replied Ackermann.

"Cavalcanti?"

Ackermann hesitated. Then he replied as if he were saying something obscene.

"Dead."

"Yvonne Klein? Henry?"

The names did not appear to produce the slightest reaction in Ackermann. Bruno made up his mind that Ackermann, despite his young and rosy face, was hopelessly senile.

"Jenny Holländer?"

"You'll be able to see her in a few days' time. We've given her a fine new spine."

"Why the hell aren't there any windows here?" cried Bruno. "Aren't I going to be rehabilitated? Aren't I going to be rehabilitated to"—he had to think to remember the year—"to 2022?"

Ackermann placed a soothing hand on Bruno's shoulder. Bruno saw that something was causing a bulge under Ackermann's coat in the armpit on his left side.

"'Hell,'" said Ackermann. "How nice to hear one of the old words."

"What does one say now, then? Do *you* know the new language?"

"Do I know the new language? How do you think I could work here actively without knowing the new language?"

"What's 'hell' in the new language?"

Ackermann pondered.

"There isn't an exact equivalent, I don't think."

"Isn't there a single person, apart from yourself, who speaks the same language I do? The old language?"

Ackermann looked offended. "Why?"

"It's not much fun with only one man to talk to. Why has the language been changed, anyway?"

142

"The old language gradually became full of meaningless words. Boring words, which just upset people."

"And yet you seem to like speaking the old language with me."

"And other patients. It's a kind of sentimentality. We shall probably teach you the new language. With this thing."

Ackermann touched the object in Bruno's armpit.

"Are magazines written in the new language?"

The question was obviously too involved to make an answer possible, but the word "magazine" seemed to waken several sentimental memories in Ackermann.

"Why don't you answer?"

"Because I think you should meet your friend with her new spine before we tackle all these problems. Tell me: did you really get to know her in the few days you were in my department—before we agreed that you should go down and await further developments?"

"I met her the day before I discovered I was sick."

"What a curious coincidence. And now you still think about her all the time, so long afterward—in fact, are living for seeing her again?"

"Yes."

"Astonishing. We gave you Obliviol to get you to forget, but that preparation is obviously still far from faultless. I'm afraid we also gave some Obliviol to Miss Holländer at various times."

"You remember me. Have you had . . . Obliviol?"

"I'm a doctor. We can't afford the luxury of what is called a *tabula rasa*."

"Obliviol—is that a pill?"

"There aren't pills any more. Obliviol is a radio wave, which we send into that little receiver in your armpit. We can strike very accurately. It's no surprise to me that you can remember magazines. It is, after all, a field you will find use for again in your new life. But we had hoped to strike certain other centra. In theory, we are supposed to be very good at striking the centra that give our patients nothing but worries. We had in fact hoped to strike that centrum which is called Jenny Holländer. Normally we strike very accurately. We were pretty sure that we had struck the centrum which is called Jenny Holländer."

"Do you know that you're senile? Do you know that you repeat yourself?" cried Bruno.

Ackermann hesitated.

"Do I repeat myself?"

He got up and walked around the cubical windowless room, the walls of which glowed green.

"I know. I'm in need of decalcification and several spare parts, but the waiting time grows longer and longer. Don't let it frighten you. My professional centra are intact and at their best age. That little habit of repeating myself is a fault that can be put right as soon as we get our electronic apparatus in order again. That little habit of repeating myself they've promised to fix in the near future. My professional centra are intact."

"Aren't there any other people at all who speak the old language?"

"We have a few. But you won't rob me of the pleasure of keeping the old language alive with our daily conversation, will you?"

"I want to talk to someone else. Can't I have a book? Can't I have a picture on the wall or hear a piece of music?"

"Naturally you can. But first I think you must meet your little friend, whose name escapes me for the moment."

"Jenny Holländer."

"Exactly."

144

Ackermann left and Bruno lay in his bed, the same old kind of bed as in his first two life periods. He missed the grating in the ceiling with its endless music, he missed books, windows, a watch that would measure out the hours until he was to meet his thawed and Obliviol-treated Jenny. As he lay on his bed, the light went out for a moment, but it soon came on again. During the days that followed, it kept going on and off but never for so long that someone came to him with a candle.

"Why does the light keep going on and off?"

Bruno had forgotten that the nurses did not understand a word of his language. He tried to find a symbol for the light going on and off, but they did not understand. He received his food regularly and it was similar to what he had received in his previous biological life period—green, brown and red blocks of a soft edible material in three flavors, which could be cut up with a plastic spoon. He was not taken out of the room when he was to be washed, but he was brought a plastic bath which he could sit in if he drew his knees up under his chin. One day, during his bath, the nail of one of his big toes came off. The whole nail floated up to the surface of the water in the bath.

"Quite natural," said Ackermann, when Bruno complained. "Minor injuries cannot be avoided in the freezing and thawing-out processes. It's quite normal. We're quite used to minor things like a nail coming off. Be grateful that it was nothing worse that fell off. Minor injuries cannot be avoided. Something like a nail that gives out is a small price to pay. Be grateful that it wasn't anything worse giving out."

The nail on his little toe also fell off, but the rest of his nails remained where they were. Bruno avoided mentioning the little-toe nail so that he would not have to hear the same soothing explanation from Dr. Ackermann in a lengthy series of variations. He worriedly watched the surface of the water in his narrow bath, but no more nails were floating on it. The nurses in charge of his bath looked like all the others and he did not attempt to learn to differentiate between them. The knowledge that they were near him while he was having a bath occasionally aroused a weak erotic mood in him, but he did not follow it up. Many days went by and he remembered that Ackermann had long ago promised him a meeting with Jenny Holländer. Had Ackermann's senile brain in his young body forgotten? It had not, for one day the light went on and Ackermann came over to his bed.

"Tomorrow it's going to happen. Tomorrow you'll be seeing your little friend," he announced, as he pressed Bruno's ankle through the bedcover, which suddenly made Bruno remember his very first stay with Ackermann, the days before he was placed in a position of choosing between living for a short while or being frozen down.

Bruno could not sleep after the light had been extinguished. Her name and the picture of her face kept him awake. It was his last chance, he thought vaguely; the cool little object under his arm ticked excitedly.

17

"You've lost a nail," said Ackermann, when he came to get Bruno the next morning.

"Two, to be exact."

"You're lucky. Not everyone gets away with just a nail. We'll give you a synthetic nail, and not a soul will know the difference."

Bruno had just finished his morning bath in the rather cramped bath made of some kind of green plastic material. The nurse handed him a comb, which he ran through his hair. As on other mornings, quite a bit of hair remained in the comb.

"Today is the day," said Ackermann. "Your little friend is waiting for you."

Then the door was opened for Bruno, and Ackermann allowed him to slip out into a short green hall. The walls were covered with something that looked like, but did not feel like, silk wallpaper. When Bruno ran his hand over the wall, he noticed that it was warm, as if elements had been set behind the silklike material, which was not soft like silk, but, on the contrary, as hard as steel.

147

"I notice that you've lost a nail from your big toe," said Ackermann, as they walked along the short passage. "That's nothing to worry about. We can give you another one which will never need cutting and won't split. We'll do something about your hair too. There's no reason why a man of your age should begin to lose his hair. But enough of these trivialities. Today is the day! You're going to meet your little friend!"

There was no one in the hall. At the end of it there were double doors, which parted as they approached. Beyond the doors was a green room that had three comfortable old leather chairs with an old-fashioned mahogany table between them, much like a card table.

"Why is everything green?" asked Bruno.

"Don't ask me."

"But we're supposed to be in the Ackermann Center? So you must know."

"The name has been changed. They didn't seem to approve of calling it after a man who was walking around alive again. Now it's just got a number. Sit down here now, and then you'll see who we can find to come and see you."

"But why green? Why not blue, like when I was last up?" said Bruno, as he sat down in one of the green leather chairs.

"The question is probably largely political. Green symbolizes hope, doesn't it? And it's soothing. Blue was the doctors' first choice. Blue is more practical and sterile, but green is the color of life, the color of hope, the color of tranquillity. That's how I interpret it, but you shouldn't ask me. Just sit back and relax."

"Does my—what is it called, in fact, this apparatus in my armpit?—does it function all the time? Sometimes it ticks and sometimes it doesn't."

"It works when it's *supposed* to work. When we find you're not calm and relaxed, or when you remember more than is good for you. Or when you actually try to *forget* too much."

Bruno sat back in the chair and relaxed, and a concept, a need he had not given a thought to in his two new lives, arose in him—tobacco.

"Could I have a cigarette?"

Ackermann smilingly shook his head.

"And mess up your fine newly cleaned lungs again? As we're talking about organs, we must remember to get you a new nail."

"Two."

"Two?"

"Two new nails."

"You asked about the colors here," said Ackermann. "As I interpret it, green is soothing and also the color of hope."

As they were waiting, the light went out, but then soon came on again. The light did not come from lamps, but it was the walls and ceiling that lit up, as in Bruno's room.

"Why is there so much trouble with the lights?" asked Bruno.

Ackermann looked up at the ceiling as if he expected the light to go out at any moment. Then he pulled a candle out of his coat pocket and placed it in the middle of the table.

"We must make sure," he said, "that we'll have a light when you meet your little friend again."

The door had closed behind them. A few minutes later, a green lamp went on above the door, which again opened. Jenny Holländer was standing in the doorway, supported by two nurses.

For a moment, Bruno was uncertain whether she recognized him. Then she smiled and his doubts vanished. With graphic clarity, two pictures appeared to him and slid into each other to become one. Jenny in the doorway after their last meeting, seen from the stairs, he on the way down, having made his decision to be frozen down. And picture number two, her face under the glass lid, which he had kissed and which had been so cold that some of the skin from his lips had stuck to it. She came toward them.

She came smiling toward them, and Bruno thought of one of the few ballets he had seen, *Coppelia*. The nurses let her go and she walked the last few steps on her own. Bruno had got up and held out his arms. With a couple of careful steps, she walked into his open arms, letting her whole weight fall against him, and he flung his arms around her. Her chin struck his shoulder and he raised his arms, took hold of her face and brought it up to his, directing it so that her mouth met his. Their lips parted, his tongue met her teeth, her teeth parted and their two tongues touched. Bruno's hands slid down her back again as he pressed her against him, keeping balance for them both. Between her back and his arm he felt something hard, a small hard object like a revolver holster, and he noticed that it was ticking gently inside the holster. He moved his hand a little and thought he felt her excited heart—or was it his own pulse, right out in his fingertips—through the shoulder blades that protruded from her back, between which, he remembered once thinking, a matchstick could be held.

One of them was crying, or perhaps they were both crying, as there was moisture between their two faces. It was not 2022, and it was not 1995. It was 1973. Time had stood still. They had been patient and now their patience was being rewarded. They did not want to lose each other again. And for the first time, Bruno thought about eternity, this eternity which had become the only thing people fought for a share in, as something more than just the opposite of dying. He thought he had chosen right when once long ago he had chosen freezing down and separation. He pressed Jenny to him, holding balance for them both, listening to the beating of both their hearts and the gentle ticking in both their armpits. And at that moment, he had forgotten the first rule of thumb of his life, that great moments should be stored away, for they contain the material for stories, stories which one can retell, distribute.

Ackermann made them sit down.

"Miss Holländer must be a little careful with her new back," he said.

"I've been given a new spine," said Jenny. "Why didn't you tell me you were going to be frozen down that day—that last day?"

"It was too involved. No one had ever heard of freezing down then."

"I couldn't understand why I never heard from you again. Someone else was living in your apartment. Someone else was in your office. Several months went by before I found out the truth."

"And you became a famous dancer?"

"Yes."

"And you had a son?"

"Yes."

"And you called him Bruno?"

"After his father."

"Where is he now?"

"I don't know."

"Professor Ackermann, can you help us?"

Ackermann came over to them.

"Your back'll be fine in a few months. As far as your nail is concerned—"

"Do you know anything about our son? About Bruno?"

"Bruno? But you're Bruno."

"We had a son. I visited him one day, on the coast."

"Did you? I'd no idea. Was he what used to be called 'now-life'?"

"Yes."

"Then perhaps he's dead. If he isn't—let me see—he must be forty-nine, an elderly man if he's not had any spare parts or eternal medicine. He could"—Ackermann smiled—"he could almost be your father!"

Bruno sought Jenny's hand under the table.

"And then you injured your back?"

"I fell and would have had to spend the rest of my life in a wheelchair."

"So you had yourself frozen down."

"Yes."

"All for your art."

"I'll dance again."

"But you had a son. We had a son."

Jenny began to cry. The light went out.

"A good thing I had a candle with me," Bruno heard Ackermann say in the darkness. A small warm flame lit up the three faces from below. Bruno got up.

"Why the *hell* does the light keep going out?"

"Don't ask me." Ackermann screened the flame to make it grow. "No one tells me anything nowadays."

Jenny dried her eyes. "I also thought," she whispered, "I also thought that if I was down long enough, then I'd meet you again."

"You didn't know any other men?"

"Yes, but I thought so much about you. And little Bruno was well cared for."

"Did you know I was up in '95?"

"I was told the other day."

"I saw you. Far down underground."

Jenny began crying gently again.

"I love you," said Bruno.

"No one tells me anything any longer," said Ackermann.

"All I know is that it's wise to carry a candle in your pocket. They keep me out of things. Disturbances, they say, if you ask questions; nothing to worry about. And the light does always come back again. But one learns to take precautions."

"You haven't changed," said Bruno.

"I love you too," whispered Jenny, drying her eyes on the sleeve of her green coverall.

Ackermann gave her a little green handkerchief and she blew her nose.

"I'm starting training tomorrow," she whispered. "My back gets better every day."

"And tomorrow we'll all three meet here again," said Ackermann. "Same time, same place. And tomorrow we'll have ten minutes instead of five. Perhaps we'll even be able to chat undisturbed by electricity cuts."

As if the word "cuts" had been a cue, the light went on again. Bruno noticed that there was a weak ticking from his armpit, and that he had hardly noticed that it had stopped.

"But I take my candle with me for safety's sake," said Ackermann.

He blew out the candle and put it back into his pocket.

Bruno pressed Jenny to him again and kissed her. Ackermann looked on smilingly, both young and paternal at the same time. Then the green light went on and two nurses came to fetch Jenny.

Bruno and Ackermann went back to Bruno's room along the short hall with its silklike wallpaper.

"I always carry a candle in my pocket," Ackermann explained. "There are some small interruptions in the current, so I've made a habit of it. I don't move a step without that candle."

18

Same time, same place, Ackermann had said, but the next day Bruno was come for earlier than he had expected.

During the previous twenty-four hours, he had experienced the awakening to life of a number of his old needs, many of them from his very first life, many of them having never appeared in his second life. There was the need to smoke. There was the need to drive a car, not just push a card into a slot and glide away, but to control the wheel himself, and the accelerator and brakes. There was the need to *buy* something, never mind what, to read advertisements and wish for things. There was the need to shave and then rub cold lotion into his cheeks and chin. Suddenly Bruno realized: My beard isn't growing; I don't shave any longer; how have they fixed that?

"Why doesn't my beard grow any more?" he asked Ackermann, as they were walking along the green hall.

"Why *should* it grow, though? For you to have the daily trouble of scraping it all off again?"

"But I'm beginning to lose my hair now."

"That's a small fault we'll soon have put right."

Ackermann did not take Bruno through the double doors at the end of the hall, but stopped at another door. An elevator took them upward. They crossed another hallway and found themselves in a room in which one wall was a mirror from floor to ceiling. For the first time in his third life, Bruno saw himself, and at his side the smiling Ackermann.

"Now you're going to see a little conjuring trick we can do," said Ackermann.

Ackermann really did look like a conjuror at that moment. He waved his hand in front of him and at this magical sign, Bruno and Ackermann vanished from the mirror, the mirror became a glass pane, and through the pane they could look into another room, a room where a young girl in green practice clothes was doing exercises by a bar. It was Jenny.

Ackermann glanced at Bruno to see if his conjuring trick had been successful. The eager young Ackermann was smiling an old man's smile, a smile, thought Bruno, like a chaperon's or a procurer's, a matchmaker's.

"Can she see us?" Bruno asked.

Ackermann shook his head smilingly. He made another magical sign with his hand and the room they were standing in was filled with the music Jenny was practicing to. Bruno recognized it. It was the mazurka from *Coppelia*. Jenny was making graceful but cautious movements. Suddenly she glided away from the bar, took a little jump, but for a moment stood immobile, as if struggling to keep her balance.

"Fantastic!" exclaimed Ackermann. "On her very first training day with a brand-new spine! In two weeks she'll be dancing better than she could ever have hoped to dance with her old one."

Jenny ran back to the bar and repeated the exercises she had begun with. Then again she glided away from the bar and pirouetted in the middle of the floor. Suddenly she

156

stopped and stood swaying there, clearly about to lose her balance, and dried the sweat from her forehead with the back of her hand. She took one step toward the bar and fell.

"Oops," said Ackermann.

Jenny got up slowly and looked around as if she did not know where the bar was.

"Miss Holländer is overestimating her strength a little. We must see that she doesn't progress too quickly."

Jenny took a step toward the bar and fell again. Ackermann again made a magical gesture and Bruno stood staring at his own reflection.

"Is there any dancing nowadays anyway?" Bruno asked. "Will she ever have any use for her dancing, even if she does learn again?"

"Even if she learns again! Of course she will. Classical ballet is timeless. Classical ballet has a constant audience."

Bruno grasped Ackermann's arm. "But magazine stories are not timeless. Admit now that magazines simply don't *exist* any more."

"All right. There aren't any weekly magazines any more. For the simple reason that there aren't any weeks any more. The decimal system has finally won, here too. But there are stories—the need for stories."

"Let me see her again."

Ackermann hesitated. Then he made his hand gesture and through the glass wall they saw Jenny, who was up again and was circling around in a long series of effortless pirouettes.

"What do you think she's thinking about?" Bruno asked Ackermann. "When she's dancing, she looks as if she's thinking about nothing at all."

"I wonder if there's time to think all that much."

"She's not thinking about me," said Bruno.

At that moment, Jenny fell again.

"Now we really must stop her," said Ackermann, making his gesture again and going over to a wall telephone to give swift instructions in a language Bruno did not understand. While Ackermann was telephoning, the music was turned off. Bruno wished violently that they would let him smoke a cigarette.

They met for twenty minutes, or about twenty minutes—though Bruno felt that he could measure time just as accurately as a clock—in the green room with the three leather chairs and the mahogany table at the end of Bruno's own hall. Jenny and Bruno embraced each other and Ackermann made them sit down.

Jenny looked depressed.

"I keep falling," she said.

"But it's only your first day, after all, Miss Holländer."

"Couldn't I at least have this thing off while I dance?" said Jenny, raising her left arm so that the object was visible.

"You'll get used to it. I never think about my own any longer."

"You danced beautifully," said Bruno.

At that moment, the light went out.

Ackermann lit his candle and placed it on the table.

"Don't worry about these little electricity cuts. Personally I've got used to having a candle in my pocket in case. Let's be grateful for a little living light."

"Who *is* it cutting off the electricity?" asked Bruno.

"Someone outside, agitators of some kind. Don't ask me, as I've long since given up trying to understand."

"Understand *what*?" said Bruno.

Ackermann did not reply.

"I danced appallingly," said Jenny. "I kept losing my balance and feeling dizzy. I'm still feeling giddy."

"What is it that you've given up trying to understand?" cried Bruno.

158

Before Ackermann had time to reply, the green lamp started winking above the door. Bruno noticed it by following Ackermann's gaze; Ackermann looked frightened.

Then the double doors glided apart and in the doorway Bruno saw a group of men. One of the men had a powerful spotlight in his hand and for a moment Bruno was blinded by the beam of light from it. When it had moved on, he saw that the men behind the man with the spotlight had weapon-like instruments in their hands. The beam of light rested on Ackermann and someone shouted something in the language that Bruno did not understand.

The rest was chaos. All three of them were taken out into the green corridor with their hands on their heads. The men shouted at Bruno things he didn't understand. He was placed against the green silklike wall next to Jenny, and Ackermann was taken away. The hall was full of men and in the light of several spotlights Bruno saw that the men were wearing yellow suits, yellow boots and yellow helmets. The elevator door was flung open and more and more men streamed out into the hall. Now they were forcing all the doors, one by one, and they brought people in green suits like Bruno's and Jenny's out of the rooms. At one moment in time, the lights went on again. It ticked weakly in Bruno's left armpit and again a man in a yellow suit forced him to put his hands on his head, directing an instrument against the little box in Bruno's armpit and pressing a trigger, with the result that the box stopped ticking. After Bruno, it was Jenny's turn. The man did the same to all of them, one after another, the whole row of green-clad people who had been stood against the walls of the hall.

Ackermann had been taken down in the elevator. The yellow men forced another door and a moment later hustled a small group of nurses across the hall and into the elevator. Bruno turned to Jenny.

"Do you understand any of all this?"

She shook her head. A yellow man came running toward them and shouted incomprehensible words at them.

Finally they were divided up into smaller groups and group after group was taken into separate rooms. Jenny and Bruno were separated from each other, Bruno ending up in a room much like his own, together with several men in green clothes like his own. The door was closed and locked behind them.

"Do we speak the same language?" Bruno asked one of the other men.

The man, who looked some years younger than Bruno, shook his head. Bruno turned to the eldest of the men with whom he had been shut in.

"You? Do you speak the same language I do?"

"I speak the old language."

"Do you understand what's happening?"

"I don't understand a thing. I think they've come to liberate us."

"Liberate us from what?"

"I've no idea."

Before Bruno could ask anything else, the lights went out. A voice shouted through the grid in the ceiling in that foreign language.

"Isn't there anyone here who can translate?" asked Bruno, when the voice stopped.

"They say we mustn't talk together," someone replied in the dark. "They say that—"

Bruno could hear no more. A whining note poured out of the grating in the ceiling and drowned the rest of the other man's explanation.

Bruno sat down on the floor. A few minutes later the whining note stopped.

"They say," someone whispered in the dark, "that if anyone says anything else, it'll begin to whine again."

There was a short whine to show they had heard him whispering. Bruno remained sitting in the dark, listening to the breathing of the others.

19

They sat in the dark, listening to each other's suppressed breathing, for a couple of hours. The whining note did not come back again. Then the light went on and a moment later the door was opened. In the doorway stood Ackermann, pale but smiling, behind him a group of nurses in their green clothes.

"I think we've persuaded our guests to leave," said Ackermann.

Bruno was the last to leave the room and to be taken back to his room.

"Jenny?" he asked.

"As right as rain. Our uninvited guests behaved pretty much like gentlemen."

"Don't you think you owe us an explanation?"

"My dear friend, if I had one, I'd give it to you."

"Has there been fighting?"

"Our guests were reduced to a minority. We used several forms of persuasion."

"But what did they come for?"

"I think they had some idea of liberating us. From what, I have no idea. Instead we were the ones to liberate ourselves from them."

"But who are we, and who are they? Are any of them doctors?"

"Renegades, perhaps. Rejected, more likely. By far the majority were presumably chance followers."

"Can't you tell me any more, or *mustn't* you?"

"I'm telling you all I know."

Ackermann took Bruno back to his room and with a sharp knife cut the binding that was holding the object fastened under his arm. Then he carefully replaced it with another one.

"Were they the people who cut the electricity?"

"They, or some other party. And now we'll send you some radio waves so that you'll have a peaceful night. We've stopped using pills and intravenous treatments. But I must have told you all about that already. You'll be getting a little wave through this and then you'll have a quiet night."

Ackermann left. In the dark, Bruno tried to remove the new box, but it was fastened as immovably as the old one. It was ticking gently and Bruno abandoned himself to a state of semiconsciousness inhabited by yellow men who directed their spotlights on him and shouted at him in a foreign language.

He woke when the light went on, to find Dr. Ackermann bending over him.

"Tell me what you remember of yesterday."

"All of it. Did you think I'd have forgotten it?"

"Naturally not. Come, we're going to see your little friend dance."

"Would you do me a favor and stop calling her my 'little friend.' We love each other."

"Exactly, and now we'll go and have a look at her while she's dancing."

Through the mirror that turned into a pane of glass, they watched Jenny practicing at the bar, setting out across the floor, starting a series of pirouettes, losing her balance and falling. She got up again and soon fell again. She got up and walked slowly back to the bar, began a new exercise, and suddenly collapsed into a heap on the floor.

"Your little friend is progressing much too fast."

A green nurse came into the room and helped Jenny up. There was a brief struggle, which ended with Jenny being allowed to continue the exercise at the bar. When the music changed and grew more lively, Jenny again danced out onto the floor and pirouetted softly, this time retaining her balance.

"She dances beautifully," said Bruno.

"She has been given the best spine you could get for love or money."

Jenny twirled effortlessly around the floor. Bruno did not understand ballet, but he could see that she had mastered the art of making what was difficult look easy. He was thinking that dancing took her away from him because he had no part in it at all. It was not the only thing that meant anything to her, but it was the most important. He wondered whether he would ever have an idea for a story again. A ballet dancer, who learns to dance with a new spine? Had that already been written hundreds of times? Did anyone write or read any longer? Were the men in the yellow suits and helmets his readers? Or the green doctors, patients and nurses? Who ruled the world outside this building he was in? *Was* there still a world of tall buildings, illuminated letters on their roofs, of boulevards and cars? Did people read in this world? The questions were too numerous and he no longer believed that Ackermann knew any of the answers.

Jenny pirouetted in one spot and fell down. Ackermann

made his magical gesture and the two men were left staring at their own reflections.

"We must persuade Miss Holländer to stick to the bar for a bit longer. We can't have her being so impatient."

Bruno turned to Ackermann.

"Couldn't I be allowed to be alone with Miss Holländer today?"

"If you mean to make love, then I think both her spine and her mind must first be more at peace. You too must have a little patience."

That day the lights did not go out during their ten minutes together in the room with the green leather chairs. Jenny seemed absent when she embraced Bruno and he recognized the slight and to him attractive odor of sweat from their very first embrace. He felt a desire to give her flowers, like the first time, and he thought about that being yet another thing he had forgotten to miss until now. Flowers. Flowers, children, tobacco, a beard to get rid of at his morning shave. Sun, clouds, the sound of rain. To be alone with a girl and make love to her.

"You danced beautifully," he said.

"Do you both watch me when I'm dancing? I don't want you to see me dancing yet. I keep getting dizzy and falling."

Bruno repeated that she danced beautifully, and that she was making progress. Jenny seemed to sink into her own thoughts. He looked at her and knew that he loved her, loved everything about her, her present absence too, hunched up in the chair, and her silence. One loves but once in one's life—one's lives—he thought, and this is your only time. It was the main point in the stories he had once given away—one great love; the fact that it might be true took him unawares. The ten minutes went by and they did not need the candle, which Ackermann once again told them he carried everywhere he went. Bruno was thinking that perhaps the yellow men and their projectors and foreign language might return and suddenly he wished that they would. When Jenny rose from her chair, she felt for a moment with her legs to gain her balance. They embraced each other again and Bruno again had the feeling that he had to hold them both upright. She overbalanced in the doorway, but was skillfully caught by a nurse.

"Why does she keep falling?" Bruno asked.

"Problems of adjustment. Try to imagine having a brand-new spine yourself."

On their way back to Bruno's room, Ackermann put his candle back into his pocket and told Bruno that he never took a step without it.

The next day, Bruno was not allowed to see Jenny dancing and their meeting was cut down to five minutes. Jenny was silent and distant and it struck Bruno that most of the time she was looking beyond him, toward the wall, as if there were something there that was very significant. When she got up, she fell forward and Bruno and Ackermann together had to help her up.

"Could one try with a completely new spine?" asked Bruno, when the nurses had taken her away. Ackermann shook his head without his usual cheerful smile.

The next day, there was no meeting of the three of them. On the following day, Ackermann came into Bruno's room and sat down on the arm of his chair. He took out a candle to show that he was prepared for all eventualities. Then he put the candle back into the pocket of his green coverall and said solemnly:

"Miss Holländer isn't very well."

"Give her a new spine," said Bruno.

Ackermann shook his head.

"It's not that. I'm afraid it's something more serious than that that's gone wrong."

"Something more serious?"

"Some misfortune during thawing. Or perhaps during her freezing period. These long freezing periods *do* have their side effects."

Bruno said something that he had been wanting to say for several days.

"The electricity cuts. Do they affect only our department? Or do they also affect the freezing departments?"

Ackermann said nothing.

"That's it, isn't it?" cried Bruno.

"The freezing departments have their own emergency generators."

"But those can be cut out too?"

"Not as far as I know."

"Once when I was down . . . is it possible that I seemed to be almost conscious at one point?"

"Impossible."

Ackermann was not looking at Bruno, and Bruno knew that he was lying.

"That's why I'm losing my hair and nails. That's why Jenny loses her balance."

"You're simplifying the causes. I didn't know you were losing your nails. May I see?"

"Only two. Tell me what you're thinking of doing about Jenny."

"Freezing her down again. She simply can't stand any longer. Don't lose heart. We're always finding new treatment. Lengthy freezing down has certain injurious effects—in certain circumstances. But developments will overtake us. In ten or twenty years' time, we'll have an effective cure for these injurious effects. In ten or twenty years' time, Miss Holländer won't have the slightest difficulty in balancing or with these depressions that trouble her."

168

"Depressions?"

"We can hardly get her to speak any longer."

"Let me see her."

Ackermann hesitated. "All right. Come with me."

"Couldn't I have a cigarette first?"

"I thought we'd talked that one out. There *aren't* any cigarettes in this building."

Jenny was lying on her back in her bed, staring up at the ceiling.

"I can't stand up any longer," she said.

"Let me hold you."

"I can't stand up, and I can't dance at all."

"And you couldn't live without dancing?"

Bruno felt that she was looking right through him.

"I want to be frozen down again. In ten years' time they can give me treatment so that I can dance again."

"Ten or twenty," said Ackermann.

"I shall be forty-three in ten years' time," said Bruno.

"Will you?" said Jenny, looking at him as if he had said something that had nothing to do with the subject at all.

"I want to be frozen down," she said. "Until I can dance."

"We are having a severe crisis of mood," explained Ackermann, feeling in his pocket to see whether he had remembered his candle.

"May we be left alone for a moment?" asked Bruno. Ackermann went out, but left the door ajar.

"I love you," said Bruno.

"I love you too," said Jenny, looking at her hands. "But I can't stand up any longer. Couldn't you wait for me?"

"Wait?"

"The ten years. Or twenty."

Bruno bent over her and kissed her. The box under his arm ticked discreetly.

"Once I saw a ballet," he said, "about a man who wakes a girl up with a kiss."

"And gets her to dance!"

"But it signified something more than just her dancing. They danced *together*. It meant that they loved each other."

Jenny looked down at her hands again, and began doing exercises with them to keep them supple.

"I saw another ballet too. About a man who falls in love with a mechanical doll."

"Coppelia!"

"But she was only a doll. You're *not* a doll."

"Coppelia," whispered Jenny, looking right through Bruno.

He kissed her again and it really did seem as if he were kissing a doll. They had done something to her, or she must always have been like that. Did he know her at all, or had she just been his pretext for going through with two freezings—his pretext for demanding *his* eternity? Had they made him into a doll too?

He was trying to find something final to say to her and a stream of magazine remarks went through his head. We'll meet again. You've never loved me. I'll always love you. Exit lines. To be continued. But he no longer believed in continuations. Without a word, he rose and walked across to the door.

At the door, he turned around and looked at her for the last time. She had already forgotten he had been there and was sleepily looking at her hands, which she was keeping supple. Outside the door, Ackermann grasped Bruno's arm.

"Do you understand now? We can't control her depression any longer. We can do nothing except freeze her down and hope for better times—put our trust in the future. And believe me, we'll find a cure. Ten years, twenty years. At worst, thirty or forty."

They froze her down that evening. Bruno stood looking at

his comb, which was full of hair. For a moment, the light flickered, but it did not go out. He lay down on his bed and had one wish only, that the light would go out and never come on again. He had not understood the yellow men and their brief action in the building. He had not understood a word of what they had shouted, but he had felt that they had taken his side. Like Jenny he stared at his hands and wished only that he could be allowed to disappear.

20

"But we've just brought you back to life! You're thirty-three, in the prime of your life!"

"Couldn't I be divided up? Isn't there any use for my parts?"

"There's no longer a shortage of parts. If we are short of anything, we make them much better synthetically. But that has nothing to do with it. Society has invested millions in you. Are they now—are they now going to be thrown away with the bath water? *Everyone* has these depressions after thawing out and preliminary shock treatment."

Bruno repeated that he wanted to die.

"There's simply nothing *called* dying. If we had the slightest reason to freeze you down again, then perhaps it could be done. But you've . . . let us just say sponged off society for half a century. Now you owe society some return in the form of work."

"*What* work?"

"We're still trying to find that out. But first you must understand one thing, and that is that you've had special treatment, an extra freezing down, because you were one of the first to trust us to have you frozen down. But now there'll be no more special treatment."

"Now it's all-life for all the money? All-life and hard work?"

"What was that word you used?"

Bruno realized that Ackermann no longer clearly remembered the words that had belonged in 1995, "all-life" and "now-life." Ackermann had been unusually clear for a few minutes, but now he was beginning to repeat himself again. He explained in every way possible that society owned Bruno, that Bruno was in debt to society and that the time had come for him to begin repaying his debt.

"Aren't there any other doctors that I can talk to?"

"You were my first patient. My first successful freezing. Do you think I would just hand you over to any young colleague?"

Ackermann appeared deeply hurt.

"I understand as well as anyone that it was a disappointment over Miss Holländer. But we can no longer promise patients simultaneous thawing. From now on, everyone must come up when he or she is in physical shape to do so. As far as your hair is concerned, then, in a short time you'll find that not only has it stopped falling out, but also what you have lost will grow again. There's simply no longer any reason why you should be down. It's unethical in a world that is screaming for labor."

"I don't want to be down. I want to die."

"Which is even more unethical. And besides, it is just a passing thawing symptom which we'll soon be able to clear up."

Ackermann left Bruno to himself. Bruno looked around the room. There was nothing loose in it that he might use to injure himself. When his food came, it consisted of soft blocks that could be eaten with his fingers, not even a plastic spoon to go with it. Bruno left the food, although he was hungry.

"Hunger-striking," said Ackermann, after Bruno had left his

174

food for twenty-four hours. "You might as well give it up. When you're weak enough, you'll get a tube in your arm for liquid food. No one has yet slipped out of the twenty-first century in *that* way."

Bruno did not touch the food. In his solitude, as light and darkness alternated, he felt a kind of solidarity growing with the yellow men who had occupied the hospital corridor. He did not know what they were fighting for, whether they were doctors, patients, all-life, or now-life, or they had yet another, fifth cause. He did not understand their language. He had always felt solidarity with the system under which he had lived, or perhaps he had never really felt solidarity with anything at all. But now he felt solidarity with the yellow men, who had some kind of change in mind. It was the first serious commitment of his life, a commitment to the unknown, a commitment to change, regardless of what change. The word became magical when repeated to himself. Change. Change.

"You wish for death," said Ackermann. "Do you understand what death means? Death is man's last enemy. We have built up a society that is based on one value only—life. When I took my Hippocratic oath in the far distant past, I committed myself to that value."

"But it's no longer life that you believe in," said Bruno. "It's eternity. The two things have nothing whatsoever to do with each other."

"They are one and the same thing. Give us a chance to prove it to you."

"You talk about society. But I don't believe a society exists any longer. Do you know that I haven't seen a window in my new life?"

"Window?" said Ackermann, as if he had to make an effort to remember the meaning of the word. Then he smiled.

"Of course you've seen a window. You saw your friend dancing through a window. You'll soon be seeing many more windows, as soon as you've got over this crisis, as soon as you have come to terms with eternity, which probably can be a little frightening, but which despite everything frightens healthy people less than death. Eat your food now and try to gain strength to come to terms with eternity. Others have done it before you."

Bruno flung the plate of soft blocks of green, brown and red food against the wall. Shortly afterward, there was a gentle ticking in his armpit and he fell into a light sleep, filled with dreams of the food of his youth. Aromatic grilled steaks, green beans and sugar-browned potatoes, long-necked wine-glasses, fat bowls of fruit, steaming coffee and large cigars, a hand curling around a brandy glass, warming its contents. Ice cubes clinking against a cold glass of whiskey and hissing soda, boxes filled with chocolates, misty bottles of beer. Music, books. Walls with bookshelves and paintings. Windows that opened, air that streamed in from outside. Sunlight and the sound of rain. The pictures repeated themselves like a film in a loop. Steaks, the smell of roast meat, endless series of meals, fragrant revelations of beauty, conversations over a tableful of friends, clinking glasses and forks, glasses that are filled, dishes changed . . . When he woke, he again hurled his food away. The next time he woke up, he was tied to his bed and a tube was fastened to his wrist. He noticed that his feeling of hunger was slowly fading away.

"Listen to me," said Ackermann. "You're thirty-three and there's no reason why you should ever be any older. You're in the prime of your life and we have given it to you. You'll still be thirty-three next time we call Miss Holländer up and can solve *her* problems."

Bruno wanted to shout much louder than he heard himself able to.

"Do you know you're hopelessly senile? Do you know that you keep repeating yourself?"

"I'm just waiting for some treatment that will clear that up. Don't you understand that just that word 'hopeless' has become superfluous? It simply doesn't exist in the new language. Nothing is hopeless. What we can't achieve today we can achieve tomorrow. Your depression. Miss Holländer's problem of balance."

"Do you live here in the hospital?" asked Bruno.

"Hospital?" repeated Ackermann, frowning as if trying to remember a forgotten word.

"Here in the center?"

"The center?"

"Have *you* got a window?"

"That word 'window' seems to play a rather special role for you."

"Window. Mirror."

"All those things exist. But they don't help us to get you back into a good mood again."

"Tell me something that helps."

"Eternity. The hope of eternity. The hope, in your case, of meeting Miss Holländer again."

"In twenty years' time."

"Twenty years has become a short time. Eternity has liberated us from our anxiety about time."

"Not mine. I'm frightened of time. I'm frightened of eternity."

"Which is a well-known symptom of the minor crisis we all have to get through. I myself have been through that crisis."

"But I don't want to get through it. I want to die."

"The longing for death is part of mortal man. Mortal man longed for death because he feared death. Mortal man also longed for eternity and invented paradise, the eternal life.

Driven by our dread of death, we've created this paradise, this eternal life. Our final problem is to get used to eternity."

"Do you know that you're standing there contradicting yourself? Is there *really* no one else I can go and talk to?"

Ackermann went out and for a while Bruno thought he had gone to get someone else, but he soon realized he was to be left alone again. He lay looking at the tube that carried nourishment into his wrists. The tube came out of a kind of plug in the wall. Bruno could not move his wrist, but he could still raise his head sufficiently that his chin rested on the tube. He drew back his head as far as he could and with all his strength jerked it at the tube. This hurt his wrist, but also meant that the tube had given a little; a little more protruded. Bruno tried to get the tube into a loop around his neck, but could not. Instead he jerked his neck against the tube over and over again, achieving nothing but soreness around his Adam's apple.

Exhausted, he laid his head back on the pillow and tried to count as he held his breath. There was a ticking in his armpit and he fell into a deep sleep.

When he woke again, Ackermann was bending over him.

"Would you like to be frozen down again?" he asked.

Bruno shook his head.

"Frozen down. And thawed out when Miss Holländer will be coming up next time?"

Bruno was silent for only a moment before shaking his head again.

"We don't care for that either. Every freezing down and thawing out brings new problems. But that's the best we can offer you. We have our Hippocratic oath to keep to, and you are our earliest patient—one of them. Unfortunate that we should have struck a person with such marked suicidal tendencies. Can't we cooperate at *all?*"

178

"No."

"All right. Freezing down."

"No," cried Bruno.

"Yes," said Ackermann, gently. "But let me frighten you a little first. We daren't go down so deeply any longer. We daren't go deeper than a kind of semicoma. Hibernation does not produce these aftereffects, these depressions. But it has its own problems. Certain functions become resistant to the chilling process. Consciousness, for instance. I name that deliberately to frighten you, as I would prefer not to freeze you down again. But if you *won't* cooperate, then that's my only alternative. Hibernation with the risk of some consciousness resistance. A certain conscious life, at a low level. Brief conscious lapses which repeat themselves like a film in a loop. Pleasant, or perhaps not so pleasant."

Ackermann went out and Bruno again tried to strangle himself with the tube to his wrists and to hold his breath as long as he was able. Ackermann appeared again.

"Semicoma," said Ackermann. "The deepest we dare give."

And he gave a series of instructions in a foreign language to the two nurses who were putting Bruno's bed on wheels.

The bed was rolled along the green corridor and taken down in the elevator. Bruno lay hoping that the yellow men would make their way into the building at this moment, that the light would go out, but the light did not go out and on a floor far down below Bruno's, he was pushed straight across a hall into a room that was of the size of his own and green once again. For the third time in his life, someone approached slowly from behind and a mask was placed over his face.

"Count, so that we can hear when you've gone," said Ackermann's voice somewhere behind Bruno.

Bruno began to count.

21

It is still light as he fastens his skates on, but dusk soon falls. He did not go out on the lake alone, there are several other skaters, but when he looks around, he sees that they have gone. He has reached the middle of the lake more quickly than he had expected and now nearly all the light has gone. He stops and looks around. He is alone on the lake. When he starts off again, he hears the ice cracking under his skates. He had wanted to cross the lake, but stops because he sees something dark in front that looks like a hole. Better to go back the same way, he thinks, then turns and sees that there is a hole behind him too. He cannot have come that way. He chooses another direction and skates for a while before he sees another hole in front of him. When he stops again, the ice cracks even if he stands still. Now there are holes on all sides of him and the last light vanishes swiftly. He can no longer see the shores of the lake. He skates on a bit in one direction and stops because the ice is cracking more loudly than before. He skates in another direction and it cracks even louder. He skates close to a hole and feels the ice just about to vanish under his skates. He stops and hears the ice creaking and snapping on all sides. Skates and stops. Each time he stops, the ice gives way a little more beneath him. He skates and stops. It is no use stopping at any one place. There are holes on one side and holes on the other. There are holes in front of him and holes behind him. The ice holds only when he keeps on skating. He keeps on skating and listens to the thin creaking ice. Avoids a hole, and then soon avoids another one. Slides past one hole after another, closer and closer to the dark edges of the holes, quicker and quicker. He can no longer reach the shores of the lake. The lake no longer has any shores. It's a question of keeping in motion all the time and steering around the holes. One must watch out.

Someone shouts *Louder* and he replies *Twenty-six*, because they have told him to count, but then he is not counting any more.

It is still light as he fastens his skates on, but dusk soon falls. He did not go out on the lake alone, there are several other skaters, but when he looks around, he sees that they have gone. He has reached the middle of the lake more quickly than he had expected and now nearly all the light has gone. He stops and looks around. He is alone on the lake. When he starts off again, he hears the ice cracking under his skates.

They do not shout *Louder* to him any more, so he does not count any longer although he could easily have counted twenty-seven. There are holes on all sides and he glides close by them as he listens to the ice cracking every time the skates strike it. It's a question of not stopping for a moment. The lake no longer has any shores. There are no longer shores one can hope to reach. A hole to the right, a hole to the left; he steers in between them. It's a question of not stopping for a moment.

It is still light as he fastens his skates on, but dusk soon falls. He did not go out on the lake alone, there are several other skaters, but when he looks around, he sees that they have gone. He has reached the middle of the lake more quickly than he had expected and now nearly all the light has gone. He stops and looks around. He is alone on the lake. When he starts off again, he hears the ice cracking under his skates.

It is still light as he fastens his skates on, but dusk soon falls. He did not go out on the lake alone, there are several other skaters, but when he looks around, they have gone. He has reached the middle of the lake more quickly than he had expected, and now nearly all the light has gone. He stops and looks around. He is alone on the lake. When he starts off again, he hears the ice cracking under his skates.

It is still light as he fastens his skates on